# Dynamo

*Also by Tariq Goddard*

Homage to a Firing Squad

Tariq Goddard

# Dynamo

SCEPTRE

Copyright © 2003 by Tariq Goddard

First published in Great Britain in 2003 by Hodder and Stoughton
A division of Hodder Headline

The right of Tariq Goddard to be identified as the Author
of the Work has been asserted by him in accordance with the
Copyright, Designs and Patents Act 1988.

A Sceptre Book

1 3 5 7 9 10 8 6 4 2

A CIP catalogue record for this title is available from the British Library

ISBN 0 340 82148 5

Quotation from
'Motto' by Bertolt Brecht, taken from *Poems 1913–1956*, translated
by John Willett and Ralph Manheim. By kind permission
of Methuen Publishing Ltd.

Typeset in Sabon by Palimpsest Book Production Limited,
Polmont, Stirlingshire

Printed and bound in Great Britain by
Clays Ltd, St Ives plc

Hodder and Stoughton
A division of Hodder Headline
338 Euston Road
London NW1 3BH

To John Stubbs and in memory of
John Carthy (1964–2002)

In the dark times

Will there also be singing?

Yes, there will also be singing

About the dark times.

**Bertolt Brecht**

# Chapter One

_Moscow 1938_

It was Monday afternoon and Radek had been woken up by love. Without hope he leant over and let his hand rest on her side of the bed. The light in his room was already turning dark violet and outside he could hear the snow sweepers call cheerful obscenities to one another. He had lost another day, and for what? The eyes he could see, and the face they belonged to, were no longer with him. The snowy crispness of late October was moving through his room and he was alone. To get up now was out of the question. The fading daylight, and the chanceless sky that bequeathed it, were already telling him that it was possible to carry on in this way for ever and that, in the end, it would mean nothing. He would never see Katya again.

It was all down to Radek now. Copic took off his glasses and shook his head. At six foot six and one hundred and eighty pounds, with healthy red cheeks and bright narrow eyes, Radek did not conform to many people's idea of a love-struck introvert but, Copic conceded, this was exactly what his star striker had become. Unfortunately, for both Radek and the rest of his teammates, Copic had very little experience of dealing with young men in situations such as this. After all, Copic had lost both his parents early in life – his brother during the Civil War, a sister in the Great Famine of 1933, two sons to the secret police, and his wife in the cholera epidemic earlier that year. Never, in the midst of all this loss, had he ever raised his suffering to the level of a complaint. Radek, on the other hand, had barely even announced his presence on the pain register, but was already playing up like a bereaved gorilla, without the slightest thought for dignity or composure. But this, in itself, was not the principal reason for Copic's anger. What really drew his ire was not that Radek had a broken heart, but rather the way in which the young Pole *could not help having one*.

The blame for this lay squarely, in Copic's opinion, with Radek's middle-class Krakow upbringing. It was the comforts of this cherry-orchard childhood which had set the tone of Radek's obsessions, encouraging pointless self-examination and whims over iron self-discipline and an adherence to duty. Both of the boy's parents had been teachers of literature and he had undoubtedly been loved to the point of suffocation, which was why now, at the age of twenty-four, Radek was incapable of closing down a part of his life, his capacity to love and be loved, and directing his energies towards another equally important part, creating and scoring goals for Moscow Spartak. And yet . . . and yet Radek was still his star striker, discovery and protégé.

'Radek, eh?' Copic growled out of the corner of his

mouth, a light shower of spittle acting as the non-verbal accompaniment to his speech.

'Training was a piss-poor shambles without him,' replied Tomsky, his assistant manager, the tone of his voice reflecting the lack of interest in his eyes. The topic was one that was beginning to bore him.

'*Training was a piss-poor shambles without him,*' Copic sneered back, his face turning purple with a sudden, but as yet suppressed, rage. 'I don't give a bent sailor's shore leave if training came off like an Olympic showcase held in honour of the Boss himself,' he roared. 'I don't even care if Radek never turns up to train again so long as he's fit to play on Saturday,' he continued, warming to his theme. 'And that's where I'm going to need your help, so get your bony thumb out of your arse and take it, along with the rest of your work-shy body, over to his place . . .' Copic paused for breath. 'And start using those much-trumpeted diplomatic skills you're always blathering on about to me . . .' His voice trailed off under the strain; he was tired after a day of shouting and his office was starting to grow cold. 'An endless shower of shit, that's what I have to contend with,' he muttered, shaking his head.

Tomsky, used to his boss's sudden fluctuations in temper, rubbed his chin and made a face, which he hoped would indicate the right amount of solidarity with Copic's predicament. Up until that weekend he, like the others, had followed the ups and downs of Radek's love life with quiet amusement, and his ascendancy as a footballer of genius with awe, but the players' dinner on Saturday night had put an end to this agreeable consensus.

Radek had broken down over his sausages and cabbage, gravy dribbling from the sides of his mouth, and pounded his fists on the table until there was silence in the room. Clumsily, he had staggered to his feet, and announced, through the laughter, his decision to retire from the game until he had won back the heart of his beloved Katya. Copic had had to be revived with smelling salts, some of the older players had joked that they would not kick another ball for the club until they had won back their virginity, and Tomsky had laughed until he shat his breeches. The only problem was that Radek had made good on his promise and had not been seen at training, or anywhere else, for the past two days.

'Cheer up, boss, we've other players in the squad . . .' Tomsky sighed laconically as he rocked back on his chair and drained the last of his vodka. For an assistant manager and first team coach, team affairs played a worryingly small part in Tomsky's list of priorities.

'The problem won't be in getting him out, we can fix that easily enough, it's in getting the bugger to *play*', muttered Copic, trapped in the single-mindedness of his thought and oblivious to his assistant's intervention. 'It's getting him to play, that's where the problem is . . .'

In the far corner of the room Muerta Astro, who had been eyeing Tomsky hungrily for the past half-hour, put down her pencil and uncrossed her legs. Her newly issued uniform, a close-fitting air force boiler suit which exaggerated her pointy breasts, and only slightly subtler buttocks, had so far failed to provoke either comment or interest. Not only was this unexpected, it was something of an outright shock, as Tomsky, since Muerta's arrival as team secretary earlier that month, had made little secret of his desire to bed her. She had not expected this to take too long, the team dinner that weekend at the latest, but instead the whole thing with Radek had blown up and since then no one, not even the lusty Tomsky, had had time for anything else.

Over on the other side of Red Square she could see the hard white lights of the Dynamo office winking out. The glowing windows reminded her of those she used to gaze at years earlier from the warmth of her father's cart, as her parents, with thousands of other hungry strikers, marched through the wealthy suburbs of Barcelona, back to their small pit villages in the foothills of the Pyrenees. She would look into those houses and pick out the rooms used by the children of the rich, with their pine bunk beds and ornately lit tapestries, and wonder what it would be like to take part in the lives that inhabited them.

Muerta picked up her pencil and began to chew it longingly. Light after light was going out in the Dynamo building, and yet here were Tomsky and Copic, slugging vodka from the bottle and expecting her to take notes, which would never be read, of the 'meeting' in progress. The lights, and the dark night that had formed around them, were inducing a homesickness that Muerta had learned first to avoid, and then later to live in fear of, largely because, unlike any of her other fears, this was one she could do nothing about. She would never see her home again.

'All I'm trying to do is tell you that we're not some one-man team . . .'

'Do you really think I don't know that already? This is *my* team, and they're *my* lads. I know everything there is to know about them . . .'

'Of course you do, and that's why I'm reminding you that Radek isn't our only player, he isn't even our only player who can play up front . . .'

Copic nodded cautiously, pleased to be talked out of the worst of his worries. 'I agree, but which of the others would you put up there without him?'

For the first time in forty-eight hours Tomsky smiled. Sensing a breakthrough, he grabbed the team sheet he had been sitting on and slapped it on the table.

'To start with, Koba and Slovo . . .'

To his surprise Copic's eyes narrowed and, sticking his arms out approvingly, he motioned for Tomsky to go on.

'Well, Koba is a big lad, and I know it's not our ideal game plan but all we've got to do is boot it up to him to stir things up a bit while Slovo exploits the space . . .'

'Koba is a two-penny muttonhead from Irkutsk . . . but Slovo, anything you have to say about his game interests me . . .'

'Well, to start with he can see things finish before they happen . . .'

'And what the hell is that supposed to mean, Mr Psychology?'

'I mean he can see what a goal will look like before it's set up and anticipate and predict the movement of a game like it's chess. I accept in other ways he's a little odd . . .'

'Bullshit. The kid's a fucking freak . . . no, don't interrupt me, you may not give a swollen Chink's eye for decorum but I do, so have the manners to hear me out for once . . .'

Tomsky sighed inwardly; Copic being denied his say was not a problem either of them often had to contend with.

'I tell you, that kid's impossible to get from one end of to the other. You see, a regular fuck-up like Radek I can handle, but Slovo's in a different class altogether, he's one of life's truly enigmatic shitheads. Of course, there *are* moments when he controls the game like a kite, but in others, and yes, I do mean last Saturday's, he stumbles from hole to hole like a golf-course rapist in search of his clubs. That makes him difficult to fit into any system of mine and a positive liability . . .'

Tomsky smiled wryly, sure that the big Slav meant somewhat less than a third of what he had just said. 'It's not as if I'm not open to what you're saying, boss, but . . .'

'But what?'

'He's young and doesn't know what his strengths are yet, I'll grant you that, but he's subtle, unusual and refined, he reads and predicts the game as well as either of us and, if played just behind Radek, he could provide him with . . .'

'I agree, I agree,' Copic said, waving his hand impatiently as if the matter had already been resolved. 'You're right, the responsibility might force some consistency out of him, but what if Radek isn't available to play? Who would you partner Slovo with?'

'Makhno.'

'Agreed. He's old but he's a war machine. And in a squad where every other man is a wild card or a masturbator we can't afford to be too fussy . . .'

Muerta Astro let out a chesty cough and pointed to the large oval clock hanging over the trophy cabinet. It was a hint neither man took. Copic appeared to be caught in the winding trajectory of a powerful and wholly unwelcome second wind and, as ever on these occasions, Tomsky seemed embarrassed to be the cause of it. To Muerta they looked like two men whose irony was entirely lost on each other, but in this she was wrong. Copic, ignorant of so many things, was always sensitive to the subtlety of his assistant's overdeveloped cynicism and wary of the way in which nearly every sentence of Tomsky's could be a joke. This was why it was impossible for most people to tell whether Tomsky was ever serious, but by appealing to his superior insight into players, Copic could find his way around Tomsky better than most. As such Tomsky was one of the few people Copic could rant at without fear of how his overblown rhetoric would be received.

Tomsky, for his part, had experienced many hours of Copic's excited conversation, and enjoyed talk which had veered from team tactics to Copic's fear of joining the rest of his family in the grave. These were nights that neither of the two men, for all their differences, would ever wish to discredit the memory of. After every home game they would listen to the gramophone in Copic's freshly bereaved apartment, Tomsky speaking of his time as a studio engineer in Chicago and his role as a party agitator amongst America's Negroes, while Copic held forth on the past in general. It was during these conversations that Tomsky began to suspect that Copic's larger-than-life persona, however real in part, was a mask created on behalf of a quieter and more thoughtful man than he could admit to being in public. Over time their shared love of blues records, laughter and strong drink encouraged an openness and intimacy that had allowed them first to become the firmest of friends, and then the first successful management team of Spartak, champions of Moscow and the USSR.

'I don't know how that one could have passed us by for so long.' Copic laughed voraciously. 'Fuck Radek! We'll partner Makhno with Slovo instead! That would be superb, inspired even! God knows why we didn't think of it in the first place . . .'

Muerta closed her folder, put her chair under the desk and strode past the men to the door. Tomsky got up as if to follow her but was helped down again by a friendly hand.

'So, Tomsky, you tireless old goat, who should we

play in goal now that Kaspar's gone and broken his bloody toe?'

The air on the Nevsky Prospect was light and sharp and the wind that blew through it shrill and painful. Muerta wrapped her scarf round her nose and tucked her head into her grey coat. It was still only October. If it hadn't been for the Civil War she would still have been walking through the gardens of the Catalan Hospice for Fallen Ladies. She turned her head back towards Red Square. The frozen and unfamiliar buildings of Moscow had never seemed so forbidding. And yet there was still something familiar carried over in the wind, something that made her think of and *feel* full of October. What this was she did not know, but she could sense all the passing autumns she had ever lived through fold into one another and obliterate everything in between. Happily she started to dance around the snow piles, watched by the first batch of nightwatchmen in the Dynamo building, far up above.

Tomsky pinched his freezing nose and thanked God that Copic had stopped talking and was now thinking of food. Smiling thinly, he ushered his boss out of the freezing room, turned off the overhead heater and double-locked the door. In truth Tomsky did not usually mind indulging Copic's desire for classification through the limited dynamics of a football conversation, it was his job after all, but tonight had taken the piss. There were other, more immediate problems in his life, more important even than Radek, Copic, Spartak and all the rest of it. Namely, that he had not had an opportunity to empty his load since the Radek affair had blown up, and that his crotch was, quite naturally, starting to play havoc with his judgement. Earlier that day, in practice, he had found himself admiring the well-toned athleticism of his own players in a way that he would not have wanted to share with them over a beer. The focus of his lust was, for once, very clear; if he did not fuck Muerta Astro by the end of the week he would go mad.

Not smiling at all now, he took his place next to Copic in the lift and, without touching any of the buttons, threw his head forward and groaned loudly. Copic, grinning happily at his assistant's frustration, affected not to notice and, moving Tomsky aside, pressed the relevant button. The two men stood in silence until the lift reached the ground floor, whereupon Tomsky refused Copic's offer of dinner and began the walk home to his empty flat.

# Chapter Two

Slovo had only just started to realise what he looked like. This growing awareness of himself as a physical being was unfortunately matched by his lack of identification with the role. The short bandy legs, bent shoulders, red hair and third nipple he had already allowed for, if not exactly grown used to or loved. The real problem was the discovery of his face. It was terrible to think of the number of people who had seen it and frightening to know that, whatever it was they saw there, it was always *him*.

'*Him* means *me*,' Slovo whispered into his open hand, its surface flat like a mirror. *Him* – the fat, square-headed one in team photos who pulled faces so as not to accept the reality of his actual one, the detestable fool with the unrecognisable side profile he kept seeing in shop windows or the mirror he was now looking into, and the abominable red pudding bowl that he saw on his head – all this was *him*.

*Me*, however, up until quite recently, had meant something very different. *Me* was the well-built young man of average height with interesting features and an intriguing haircut. *Me* was the one all the fans chanted for whenever a goal was created out of nothing, but most of all *me* was the man Slovo saw whenever he pictured himself in his mind's eye. It was true that sometimes *me* would try to imagine what this other face looked like, the one everyone else saw, but he could never pull it off. The task had always felt too abstract to be truly worth undertaking, rather than too terrible to contemplate the truth of.

A hapless tear of self-pity rolled off Slovo's cheek into his flask of warm milk.

Picking up the evil handle of the thick black scissors that lay on his trunk, he grabbed a handful of hair and, with controlled self-loathing, sheathed it off. Let Copic shout 'What the fuck have you done that for, deaf kid?' in training tomorrow, let him. Because he would never tell him why, not him or Tomsky either. He would never let them know that he now knew what his face looked like because he had laid eyes on little Lotya, wife of Chief Grotsky, NKVD man and manager of Moscow Dynamo, and little Lotya had looked back at him. No, he would not tell them. He would not tell either of those two animals a thing.

Copic stumbled through the door and into his little kitchen, smashing his head, as usual, on its low entrance. Roaring loudly, he aimed a couple of punches at the place where the plaster had come loose and cursed himself for not having taught it a proper lesson the last time he had banged his head there. Furrowing around the kitchen like an injured bloodhound, Copic quickly found what he was looking for – two-thirds of an old garlic sausage, half a tin of tomatoes and a quarter of turps, pilfered from the physio's medical bag. Quickly shuffling the sausage into his mouth, Copic emptied a fingerful of turps into the tomatoes, gave the concoction a little shake and downed it in one. Burping like a bastard, he hauled himself over to the sink, splashed a little water over his face, and retired towards the old bearskin rug, used on those occasions when he could not be bothered to go to bed.

Before long an expression of haunted dissatisfaction had broken across his face as, down by his tangled legs, plump little mice shuttled crumbs of garlic sausage through the darkened apartment, indifferent to its sleeping master's snores.


'The truth, my friends, is knowing what is on offer, and we, the working people of this country, are not being told the truth . . .'

Josip gazed around nervously; there could have been no more than fifteen others at the meeting held in the cramped basement apartment in the Maxim Gorky block.

'. . . Ours is not a workers' state but a bureaucratic prison house, a closed system run on behalf of the Party that claims . . .'

No, this was not what Josip had been led to expect when he had read the note slipped under his door after practice that afternoon. Instead of the Catalan émigré gathering, home cooking and old faces he was promised, he had walked into a room of highly politicised strangers in the middle of a meeting. Getting up tactfully, ignorant but still mindful of who he might upset, Josip shuffled towards the door. Unhappily he found his way blocked by a handsome woman who, he thought, would have been attractive to men had she cared about them.

'Where are you going?' she asked firmly.

Josip recoiled, angry with her for making him feel guilty.

'I'm on my way home. I've had a long day and I'm tired and . . . and I don't belong here,' he added clumsily.

'But you're from Spain and were in the CNT, and now, in my country, you play for Spartak, the workers' team.'

To his embarrassment Josip recoiled again. It felt worm-like to have grown so scared of recognition. And yet he knew he had to leave immediately, whether this woman knew who he was or not.

Pushing her gently to one side, he opened the door and was about to walk out of it when he felt a hand on his collar. Turning around to offer a quiet apology to the woman, he saw something unexpected; Nestor Makhno, his midfield partner at Moscow Spartak. Makhno winked chillingly and, without saying anything, took his place in a seat next to the woman who had accosted Josip seconds before.

For a moment Josip stood there dumbly, his body hopelessly frozen as if faced with some unperformable duty. Then, with shamefaced hesitancy, he walked back to where he had been sitting before, and took his place again beside an old metal worker.

Neither Makhno nor the woman made any effort to talk to him when the meeting ended half an hour later, which was just as well – Josip was relieved to be able to walk back to the apartment he shared with his compatriot and one-time mistress, Muerta Astro, by himself.

Josip was scared of dying in Russia. Of course, he had been scared of dying in Spain too. The collapse of the POUM, the execution of his comrades, murdering a corrupt official for false documentation and the end of the Republic had, in different ways, scared the living crap out of him. And as bad as all these misfortunes were, they suffered nothing in comparison to what followed in their wake: the horror of evacuation. Here Josip had seen mothers throw their babies into departing boats and strangers bat the babies back like tennis balls. He shook his head at the memory of how, as sinking ships fired red distress signals into the sky, he had helped his daughter remove her life jacket to wipe the sick off it, lost her in the crush, and felt the deck collapse beneath him. A whirlpool of twisted metal and burning oil had swallowed her and, like a dead man, he had held on with the other stoics, smoking their last cigarettes among the shattered lifeboats on the remnants of the deck, and waited for his turn. But the cold black water had shocked him into life, and kept him moving, so that in the end he had come to find Muerta, clinging to a crate of Valencia oranges, and joined her on board a cruiser loaded with Spanish gold bound for Moscow.

Perhaps this was why he now prized his life so highly and was so reluctant to lose it in a country where, if he thought about it all, he already felt dead. It was just the cold and fear of drowning which kept him moving.

Josip tiptoed into the flat that he and Muerta, as 'guests of the Soviet Government', shared, and knocked gently on her door. She was asleep. This was for the good. If she had been awake he would probably have told her about the meeting and thus endangered her life as well as his own. At least now he would be forced to carry his own water.

Falling on to the couch, generously donated by the miners of the Urals to the 'heroes' of Republican Spain, Josip breathed in deeply, as if he were inhaling mountain air. The whole room smelled of Muerta and, to Josip's cold nostrils, like all things feminine. In other words the opposite of the Spartak dressing room, Copic's office, and the stench of burning oil on salt water. The smell automatically made him think of sex. He looked over at Muerta's door. It was strange how he no longer desired her, especially as she had tried to seduce him earlier in the year when drunk. The urge had passed, though, and now they were happy to walk around each other like naked siblings who had grown out of incest.

With fond care he picked up one of her boots, lodged in her giant cone-shaped bra, and put it by her collection of 'rare' stones, thus giving it the appearance of an ornament. It warmed him to realise that he was living with a girl who preferred junk picked up off a beach to collecting stuffed dolls, expensive jewellery or similar tack. Sighing contentedly, and momentarily free of his worries, he cast his clothes off and, wrapping himself up amongst a huddle of Muerta's shawls, closed his eyes and began to drift.

Back across the city his friend, Boris Slovo, had finished his new haircut. To his great consternation it looked even worse than before, and his mirror image, with nothing left in the way of hair to hide it, stared straight back at him defiantly, as if to say, You've fucked it, you fool.

Hurling the mirror across the kitchen, Slovo rushed into the bathroom screaming obscenities and beating the side of his head with the heavy handle of the scissors. The sound of the mirror crashing into a pile of unwashed plates roused Kasper Hasek, Slovo's flat mate and Spartak goalkeeper, out of his slumbers and towards the bathroom door, where he found his friend in tears and as bald as a baby seal.

'My God, Slovo, what have you gone and done that for, my boy? You look as though you're ready to be transported to the gulag or thereabouts,' Kasper bleated, his tone a mixture of sympathy and disbelief. 'First Radek and now you. What's the world coming to, eh?' he went on shakily. 'Come on, let's get you on your feet, man, we can't have you sitting around on the floor like a starving peasant.'

'It's nothing, nothing, Kasper . . . please don't tell anyone, just promise me that you won't.'

'I promise, old man, I promise, but . . .'

Slovo looked at him imploringly.

'Don't you think we should do something about your hair . . . I mean your head,' Kasper said as he pointed to Slovo's box-shaped dome. 'We can hide your tears but people will ask you about your hair,' he added, hoping that this would prompt Slovo into some sort of explanation. He was to be disappointed.

Slovo looked down at his toes, and his whole face, and head, turned bright red. It was obvious to Kasper that he was not going to get anything more out of him until the morning.

'Well, there's only one thing for it, then,' Kasper said at last, 'we're going to have to get you a wig. My uncle has a place and we can fix it up and fasten it down with glue before practice tomorrow. Don't you worry, old man, you'll be as right as rain and no one will be any the wiser . . .'

One man who would be the wiser was Tomsky, who, as usual, was having trouble getting to sleep. For the past hour he had unsuccessfully attempted to settle on the image of a naked Muerta Astro and enjoy the subsequent erection. But other thoughts kept getting in the way. Most things come to those who no longer care whether they get them or not, he conceded as the sleeping pills finally kicked in and a cavalcade of Muertas descended upon him, their thousand mouths whispering softly all the while.

# Chapter Three

*Tuesday*

'We're going to be late. You should've woken me up like I asked you to, you careless bastard.'

'You don't usually like it when I do,' Tomsky replied laconically.

Copic scowled at his assistant and waved a fist symbolically. 'I don't give a weasel's jockstrap whether I like it or not, next time wake me up or face my wrath, you wretched son of a pedantic whore.'

Tomsky started to laugh and, as Copic bent down to tie his laces, stuffed a heavy ball of ice down the back of his boss's neck.

Surprisingly the red-faced Copic seemed not to notice. 'Give me a hand with these fucking laces before my fingers freeze up and . . . baby Jesus, what the hell's that dripping down into my undershirt, Mother of Kazan! Am I beset by a plague of demons?'

'You'd better tone down the religious talk before the secret police hear you, you could be facing a tenner in the camps if you're not careful . . .'

'Oh, you'd like that, wouldn't you! Old Copic out of the way so you could have the whole lousy team to yourself. Well, let me tell you something, bum boy, without Copic there's no team so . . . Hold it, my keys, where are they? I think I must have left them in the apartment . . .'

Turning on his heels, Copic rushed back into his apartment block and was at the third floor before he realised he had already thrown the keys at Tomsky when he'd first walked out five minutes earlier. Barging through a family queuing for the communal toilet he had pebble-dashed the night before, he charged back down the stairs, cursing Tomsky for rushing him and toying with his blood pressure.

'Are we all set?' enquired Tomsky as he handed Copic the keys. 'You look as though you've been in the tropics. You should keep the heat down, you're not a young man any more . . .'

'Keep the heat down! My face feels like a bucket of ferrets trying to escape a beetroot farm and you say keep the heat down! Try humouring me this morning, Tomsky, by never saying anything to me on any subject ever again, eh? There's a good lad.'

Tomsky nodded obligingly as Copic caught his breath and loosened his scarf.

'I feel like I'm burning at the stake even when it's fucking freezing,' he muttered. 'Jesus, to have my health back.'

The simple fact of the matter was that Copic was only thirteen years older than Tomsky but, to any observer, could quite easily have been thirty. Whereas Tomsky's narrow face carried a single burst blood vessel, a tiny blemish just above the nose, Copic's face was a moving network of red lines and purple patches, spread over his features like sand.

'Water, boss, you need to drink water and plenty of it. That's what'll clean your insides up. It's what we keep telling the players, after all . . .'

'Save your urine extraction programme for those who appreciate the bloody treatment . . .'

'I'm serious. I'm worried about you and your diet. All you eat is shit . . .'

'Not so worried that you'd have dinner with me when old Copic asked you to last night, eh, Tomsky? That's right, I've caught you, haven't I, you hypocritical bastard?'

'Why do you have to personalise everything? I really am trying to make a serious point about your health.'

'Listen, my boy, I'm not yet forty-eight, that's younger than bloody Lenin was before he started the October bloody Revolution. Younger than him, do you hear me!' Copic pointed triumphantly at a statue of Lenin they were walking past. 'So don't try telling me that my best is behind me . . .'

Tomsky smiled indulgently. It was difficult sometimes not to feel sorry for Copic, since, for all his bluster, there was a strange vulnerability about the man. Tomsky often found it hard to reconcile the Copic he had come to know with the man the older members of the back-room staff would reminisce about. Copic, for them, was the leader who taught his children how to read and write, who attended the Communist Self-Improvement Night School, and who came top of his class, beating even Klimt Grotsky, head of the NKVD, in his literature papers. This was a side of himself that Copic had involuntarily buried under layers of grief, or so Tomsky thought, which would at least explain the clownish repertoire that had now become his boss's calling card. Perhaps as a fundamentally simple man, Tomsky reasoned, there was a freedom in idiocy that Copic had been unable to find in the 'educated' life of a self-made working-class intellectual.

Copic made a heavenward gesture with his eyebrows and, picking up a pile of slush, wiped some over his face and threw the rest at Tomsky.

Tomsky was well protected from such an attack. He was dressed from head to toe in heavy black leather, his slim legs and narrow torso bound as if in armour plating. Copic had had a similar outfit made for him in brown but he never wore it because it reminded him too much of the uniform worn by the commissars during the Civil War. Both outfits had been gifts from the Leatherworkers Union, one of the three unions that Spartak had been set up to represent. The other two were the textiles and food workers' cooperatives.

'What time do you make it?'

'Half eight.'

'Shit. We're going to be late. As usual.'

Tuesday mornings meant a trip to the textiles mill, where Copic and Tomsky would be quizzed about their team's progress by the heads of the big three unions. Although it was a chore neither of the two men minded, Copic performed better at these occasions than Tomsky. Tomsky, distrusted slightly because of his Communist Party background, had only just started to enjoy the same 'warm' relationship with the union bosses that Copic had naturally commanded from the off.

'Come on, come on, get out of our way, we're never going to match the capitalist West by standing around dawdling all day like a pack of off-duty cops,' yelled Copic at a group of commuters.

A secret policeman scratched his ear and smiled as he watched Copic and Tomsky push their way into Moscow's newly completed Metro system. It was his job to follow the two men wherever they went, day or night, and his work was rarely dull.

'This . . . this thing is *fucking marvellous*,' uttered Copic, his voice shaking with emotion, as he pointed at the gaudy marble walls of the Metro entrance. 'A triumph of . . . of *everything*, when you come to think of it.'

Tomsky shook his head. Unlike the ebullient Copic, who considered the underground system a miraculous and futuristic pleasure, Tomsky found the Metro grim and laboratory-like. It was impossible for him not to descend the escalators without his mood becoming at one with that of the single most depressed person travelling on the system that day. Copic, meanwhile, treated it as an opportunity to showcase his public-speaking skills.

'Take the way we fucked Dynamo Tbilisi last Saturday,' he called down the platform. 'Now I don't mind telling you that there're a lot of coaches who would've lost their nerve at having gone two–nil down, most in fact . . .'

Such conversations would always arouse the interest of fellow Metro travellers who, on recognising Copic, would shower him with praise and ask to shake his hand. Again, this was something Copic enjoyed more than Tomsky.

'No, no, no, the secret of great coaching isn't understanding your players, it's getting them to do what you bloody want . . . but then don't quote me on that because people always go backwards when they think they know what they think, eh, Tomsky, eh?'

Tomsky pulled his collar up over his ears and let out a mock howl of protest. Copic, meanwhile, surrounded by a keen gaggle of admirers, chatted happily on, his words drowned out only by the sound of the oncoming train.

Radek pulled the heavy rug up over his eyes. Scattered snowflakes blew through the open window of his freezing room. He lay stretched on his bed, still and phantom-like. He would not be going anywhere today, not while he still had Katya's face to think of and remember.

'I've been thinking about our conversation last night,' said Copic as he stepped off the train and onto the salt-covered platform.

'Which part of it?'

'The part about who we get to replace old, useless Radek.'

'And . . . ?'

'Well, I've slept on it and I don't think it's possible, to replace him, I mean. I was being too optimistic when I said that it was possible to cope without him. We rely on him too heavily, and nothing I can do overnight is going to change that.'

'You're probably right about that.'

'I know I'm right, which is why I want you to take the situation in hand. I'm prepared to bet a pair of hairy bollocks that the lad won't make it into training today. So I think we should revert back to Plan A; you go over to his apartment, get inside his fucked-up head and get him playing for us. By any means you can. You have a way with people, with unhappy people anyway, that I don't. I can trust you with this, can't I? I mean, it's not as though you're that much use in training anyway.'

'Yes, I don't see why it should be too much of a problem . . .' Tomsky answered, puzzled by the ease of his own reply but keen to keep Copic in a good mood.

'Good man, good man,' said Copic as he slapped his assistant on the back. 'And I'd rather we didn't say anything about this little incident to the chiefs, eh?'

'Our secret's safe with me,' said Tomsky, tapping his nose.

'That's the spirit. There's no point in shovelling our shit up for inspection, there's enough people who want to undermine us as it is.'

'And who would you be thinking of now?'

'Why, those cunts over at Dynamo, of course.'

'Of course.'

There was a silence, the first of the morning. It was not an especially comfortable one and Tomsky was sorry he had caused it.

'By God, I hate this area,' Copic said, changing the subject.

'You say that just about every time we pass through this spot.'

'That's because it's always bloody true. This place reminds me of St Petersburg when I was a boy, another bloody shithole if you didn't have the money to go out and enjoy it properly. That's something that you "wet behind the ears" apparatchiks will never understand, Tomsky, sheer bloody poverty.'

'Don't give me that, my father worked in a factory.'

'Ah! But you never did, did you, my finely turned-out friend?' said Copic, wagging his finger.

'I don't think that really deserves a response.'

'But you haven't, have you? You've never worked in a factory and, consequently, know nothing, and I mean nothing, about real poverty,' repeated Copic, almost laughing now.

'Aren't there any other battles for you to go off and start?' snapped Tomsky irritably.

'I've got you there, haven't I?' Copic giggled as he walked straight into a newspaper seller.

'Watch where you're going, you fat pig,' cried the

boy. 'You could have smashed my feet up with those hoofs of yours.'

The boy's swollen feet were wrapped in newspaper and cloth rags. His toes were little purple bumps.

Guiltily Copic reached into his pockets to retrieve a few kopeks. Tomsky, taking advantage of his boss's indisposition, stepped to one side, mindful of his new surroundings. They had arrived in the Zenith; an area contemptuously referred to by Party members as the Vendee. It was here that the criminal underworld mixed with the poorest and most desperate sections of the working class, most of whom were factory peasants who had fled the country to escape starvation and collectivisation. It was an area that had become synonymous with suffering. Twice in the past year Tomsky and Copic had been summoned to the local workers' club to form part of a proletarian jury, on the first occasion to judge eighteen youths charged with a gang rape, on the second to convict a madman who had mutilated a pack of carthorses. Such incidents were not uncommon but they were always reported in the papers as 'foreign-inspired banditry', and the culprits would be ushered away to Siberia or shot in their prison cells.

'Fill me full of shit and turn me upside down, it's impossible to tell whether it's snow or worms guts' you're stepping in,' said Copic, wiping his boot against a heavy locked gate. 'We might as well be wading through the belly of a bloody whale.'

The snow they were walking on was brown and orange, giving the light in the street a sordid yellow tinge. Every few steps someone, to their left or right, would slip on the black ice patches and yell out in anger. After a while it began to seem to Copic and Tomsky that these performances were being enacted solely for their benefit – an inbred joke played out on strangers.

'Hard to tell whether it's day or night in this place . . .'

'Like St Petersburg when you were a boy?'

'Up yours, you mischievous villain.'

'I can't do right by you, can I?'

'Too bloody right you . . . Aaaah! Can you smell it? Can you smell it already?'

Tomsky could. The two men turned the corner and were faced with the sight, and the phenomenal stink, of the Red October Leatherworks.

From the giant medieval parapets of the factory the three great chiefs of the leatherworkers, textiles and food production unions watched the arrival of Copic with fear and growing trepidation.

'What the hell are we to say to him . . .'

'How am I supposed to know?'

'I thought we agreed that you'd be the one to tell him . . .'

'I'm damned if I can now . . .'

'Well, one of us will have to say something, he's got to know or else the heads that'll roll will be ours . . .'

\*　　\*　　\*

Tomsky walked into the office first, Copic having been stopped on the factory floor by fans and admirers.

'Welcome, Eider Ilyich, can we offer you anything to drink?'

'Anything to drink means, and can only ever mean in this place, vodka.'

'Ever the joker, Tomsky, ever the joker. Here, Zayets, fetch the good Tomsky a large vodka.'

The man addressing Tomsky was Rykhly, chairman of the food workers union and the boss on best terms with Copic; to his right was Zayets, head of the leatherworkers, and sitting in silence under the portrait of Stalin was Shkaf, leader of the textiles union, the only one of the three men whom Tomsky trusted.

'From success to success, Tomsky, from success to success. Do I even need to tell you again how proud you've made us? Judging from your face I'm not sure that I do. But still, can there be a better manager in the country than Igor Ivanovich Copic, or a better assistant manager than your good self? Well, can there?'

Realising that the question was not strictly rhetorical, Tomsky answered, 'I don't know, it's not the sort of question I'd normally think of asking myself.'

'Well, of course not. You're an artist, Tomsky, the sort of man who invents and creates things. What use could such questions be to a man like you?'

If this had come from anyone else Tomsky would have suspected irony, but Rykhly, a champion arsekisser and card-carrying hypocrite, was almost certainly in earnest.

'You'll have to forgive the enthusiasm of Chairman Rykhly, Comrade Tomsky, and remember that the delivery of ham and cheese is his business,' said Zayets, the politician of the group and a man whose career had advanced over the dead bodies of his predecessors. 'But after all, Rykhly does have a wonderful point. Since the formation of the Soviet league in 1935 you and Copic have led us to two league and cup doubles and to four derby victories over Dynamo, our Moscow rivals. Moreover you have achieved this with panache and style, playing an attractive passing game that is the talk of all Europe.'

'Bravo, bravo, Zayets, I only can only hope to aspire to your eloquence and erudition,' gushed Rykhly.

'Please, Chairman Rykhly, it is not I but our friends, Comrades Copic and Tomsky, that we should be praising. Comrade Tomsky, take your vodka and join us in a toast to yourself and Copic . . .'

'What's all this about toasts and Tomsky? That snide little backbiter trying to muscle in on my job again, eh?' said Copic as he stumbled through the door, a jug of vodka already in his hand.

Rykhly and Zayets let out a chorus of laughter, filling the room with authentic falsity. Copic joined them, his laugh that of a genuine buffoon. Tomsky looked over at Shkaf, who had been silent until now. Shkaf looked back, his eyes red and dejected. Slowly the old peasant pointed at the portrait of Stalin and shook his head. It was at this point that Tomsky feared the worst.

'Ten more years, eh? What do you say to that,

Tomsky, ten more years of the old magic, eh?' sang Copic, his mug swinging wildly over his head like an axe. 'Ten more years of the old magic!'

Pushing Tomsky to one side, the enormous Rykhly grabbed Copic's free arm and, grunting like a satisfied hippo, shouted, 'Ten more years, Igor Ivanovich, ten more years!'

'You must excuse Chairman Rykhly, Tomsky, he is like your very own Copic, a lover of life and a lover of the game,' said Zayets, his smile switching from the sickly to the sinister.

'And am I to take it that you're a "lover" of neither, Zayets?' said Tomsky, giving in to his natural urge to antagonise.

'I love only our work, Tomsky, only our work . . .'

'Come on, Tomsky, get a drink down you. You're one half of an unbeatable partnership, for Christ's sake!'

Zayets coughed. 'Comrade Copic is right, you are an *unbeatable* partnership; this *unbeatableness* being the very thing that I wish to talk to you both about.'

Rykhly let go of Copic and stepped back awkwardly. Zayets breathed in slightly and raised his chin. Shkaf groaned, his head already in his hands.

Copic was left standing on his own in the middle of the room, his mug still swinging in his otherwise still hand.

'What is this?' he said, his eyes narrowing instinctively. 'Tomsky, do you know what this is?'

Tomsky shook his head. 'No, boss, I don't.'

'Let's not be too hasty, boys, Zayets only meant . . .'

'Shut up, Rykhly, I'm perfectly capable of speaking for myself.'

'Then what are you saying, Zayets?'

Zayets breathed in heavily and looked out towards the turrets of the factory. It seemed as though no one was keen to lead Copic out of his bewilderment.

'Could someone tell me what's going on here? Is something being insinuated that I'm supposed to understand? That perhaps young Tomsky and myself are fixing matches? Or maybe bribing the ref? Is that it? Because I heard something in your voice back there and it wasn't innocent or pretty. Am I right, Tomsky?'

Tomsky nodded, ready to agree with Copic but unwilling to actually encourage him until he knew where the axe would fall.

'I'm sorry, Comrades.' Zayets laughed. 'I would have held my tongue if I had known you were so thin skinned! Here, Chairman Rykhly, give our friends another drink, hurry now, before I find some other way of offending them . . .'

Rykhly laughed weakly. The atmosphere in the room had become quite different to that of a minute earlier.

Tomsky grinned at Rykhly and, as unselfconsciously as he could manage, tried to do the same to Zayets; it was impossible. Neither of the two men returned his glance. Everybody, with the exception of Copic, who was fuming, seemed distracted by either his wedding ring or his watch strap. Tomsky sighed; this was how business was done in the Soviet Union.

'So, friends,' Zayets continued, his tone changed to that of a schoolmaster, 'your unbeaten run has certainly attracted plenty of interest from the very bottom to the top. It's virtually *unheard* of to do so well, that's all I meant. So please don't let me be misunderstood, it was never my intention to insinuate that there was something dishonest or discreditable about your triumph . . .'

'Well, hooray for that,' muttered Copic.

'. . . on the contrary, as I have already said, both of you are where you are on merit alone, which brings me to the first of my points; you and your team are the best in the country because of your natural and – I hesitate to use this word – God-given talents. And this is not something that makes everyone happy.'

Copic and Tomsky stared at each other quizzically, both of them confused as to where the conversation was going.

'Now what compounds this problem is that no one is really sure how you *do it*, least of all ourselves. You don't practise as regularly or as hard as the other teams, and even when you do your training is hardly conventional. None of your team plans or formations can be found in any of the manuals or books. Indeed, you seem to take pleasure in changing your system all the time . . .'

'That's right,' butted in Rykhly. 'I haven't seen you play the same way more than twice this season. Sometimes you have that Polish lad up by himself, then the next week . . .'

'Rykhly, you can have your say, *if you have anything to say*, when I've finished.'

'Sorry, Zayets.'

'So you don't like our tactics, then,' said Copic, able to find his voice again.

'No, no, no, no, Comrade Copic, you couldn't be more wrong. What I don't like isn't your tactics but some of the *people* who like your tactics.'

Tomsky felt a lump harden in his throat; this was becoming too bizarre even by the high standards set by the USSR.

'I don't understand this at all, Zayets,' said Copic. 'Who are the people that admire our tactics other than our fans? You're not making any sense as far as I'm concerned . . .'

'That's the nub of my point, Igor Ivanovich. You see, the ones I'm alluding to *are the fans*.'

Tomsky could not believe what he was hearing. Zayets was talking like a paid-up Party member, in other words exactly the type of person he had once accused Tomsky of being. Of course, it was possible that the Party could have got to Zayets in some way, through his family or by appealing to his ambition, but even so, why were they hearing this? What did Zayets want from them?

'Our fans . . . I'm sorry, this is like hearing a riddle in a fairy story,' said Copic, looking to Tomsky for help.

'No, please relax, Comrades. No criticism whatso-ever is being made of either of you. You have behaved like good coaches and have been busy with the team and with what happens on the pitch, that's why you manage a great team . . . but this is also why you may be less aware of other, equally sensitive matters that occur off the pitch.'

'Am I right in thinking that you're referring to rather more than just our fan base?' asked Tomsky.

'Exactly, Tomsky, "rather more" is exactly what I am referring to,' Zayets replied. 'You see, Rykhly, I told you that our Comrade Tomsky was a clever one.'

'But the fans are, if anything, more your responsibility than ours,' said Tomsky, thinking aloud in the hope of pre-empting Zayets' oblique logic. 'Most of them come from the Zenith and are employed in your factories. They're our fans and we're your team but . . .'

'Yes, Tomsky, that is true but, if you'll pardon me for saying so, not the complete truth; and therefore perhaps an untruth. Spartak are not just the team of textiles, food or leatherworkers, but of nearly *all* the workers in these slums. Not only that but they are the team of the artists, the writers and the intelligentsia – in fact of nearly anyone who doesn't support Dynamo . . .'

'What about Torpedo, or the rail workers' team Lokomotiv . . .'

'But if it comes to a derby against Dynamo, then fans of those clubs will always support us . . .'

'Then just what the hell are you saying, Zayets, that we should take greater care in alienating potential fans?' said Copic, who was starting to feel like a passenger in the conversation.

'I am simply pointing out that wherever you find dissent against the authorities in football, you'll find Spartak fans behind it. Now, I accept that Dynamo is the team of the secret police and will therefore always be supported by Party members, there is nothing we can do about that for the moment . . .'

'Since when have you had such a soft spot for Party members, Zayets?'

'Comrade Copic, please, such talk is indecent and wrong headed!'

Tomsky and Copic shared a horrified look. Now they *knew* something was wrong. Zayets may have been an opportunist and backbiter but he had never been a prude or Party yes-man.

'Zayets, if you're asking us to take this meandering sermon seriously you'll have to hurry up and get to the point because at the moment neither of us has any idea what you're talking about.'

'I'm surprised an intelligent man like you can't see how each point hangs together as a whole,' said Zayets, addressing Tomsky. 'Let us look at your situation again, shall we? Here you are, two mavericks leading a team of independent-minded individualists to victory after victory in the first communist country in the world, a country that values the collective over the individual and stealth over flair. Do we notice anything odd yet? Do I need to continue? Oh well, I'll continue, then. Not only does this team beat, and is seen to beat, the one team that encapsulates the Soviet ethic in sport, both in terms of composition and method, namely

Moscow Dynamo, but your team then becomes a public meeting point for any type of subversive wrecker with a grudge against the Party or regime . . .'

'Fuck me, Zayets, have you been rehearsing this in front of the mirror with a glove puppet? I've never heard such bollocks in all my life. What do you say, Rykhly? Don't tell me you're ready to take any of this squirrel crap seriously.'

Rykhly started to wobble like a plate of jelly. 'I'm sorry, Igor Ivanovich, you know how much I love you and your wonderful team . . .'

'That's not what Copic asked you, Rykhly,' said Zayets. 'Tell our friend what you told me earlier. Word for word, now, do you hear me?'

'Yes, yes, I hear you, Zayets,' wavered Rykhly. 'They say, Comrade Copic, that in the camps Spartak games have become a tolerated form of dissent, that they are the one place where criminals and political prisoners can gather by the radio and cheer on your side, giving open expression to their hatred of our Motherland . . .'

'. . . and to communist values in general. And for what it's worth I'm sure you'll agree that the situation isn't much better inside the stadiums either,' concluded Zayets.

'I can't believe that I'm hearing this piss!' shouted Copic, all sixteen stones of him shaking with anger. 'Do you hear this, Shkaf? Don't tell me they've driven you mad as well?'

'What *can* you say to such shit, Igor Ivanovich?'

The former peasant shrugged. 'But then I'm an old man now, I've heard their lies many, many times before . . .'

'You leave Shkaf out of this, Copic; our old comrade is tired and in bad need of a long holiday. What you should be concentrating on is how you'll answer to the charge of helping to facilitate the creation of a sporting elite.'

'You must be joking, Zayets, this is too much,' said Tomsky, scared that if Zayets were allowed to go on talking things would probably get even worse. 'Now listen to me, I was in the Communist Party long enough to know that wherever there's a problem there's usually a deal . . .'

'But of course, Tomsky, so perhaps we'll get down to some business now and begin the conversation proper . . .'

On a nearby step sat the secret policeman. He checked his watch and compared the time with that on the clock hanging above the acres of cow hide stretched over the factory floor. There was no doubt about it – they were certainly taking longer than usual today. Slapping his hands together, he stood up and walked towards the boiler room in order to keep his feet warm. It was funny how some people enjoyed talking so much, especially as it did them so little good in the end.

Copic's face had turned the colour of an overripe grape.

He held a hand to his forehead and gasped, 'I need to sit down.'

'Zayets, fetch Comrade Copic a chair and a glass of water.'

'I can't believe you're asking us to do this.'

'It's no easier for us than it is for you, Tomsky, but, when you look at the facts, is this really worth losing your life over?'

'He's right, Comrade, it's only a game, after all.'

'For you maybe, Rykhly, but for us it's something rather more than that.'

'But nonetheless, when compared to your life . . .'

'So let me get this right, Zayets, you want us, in the interests of fairness, to lose our game against Dynamo this weekend . . .'

'No, not lose, Comrade Tomsky, just not win, and it's not me that wills this but, as I have already said, a far higher authority . . .'

'. . . *you* want us to throw this game because it's not *fair* that we win so often, but the team we have to lose to can't be Leningrad, Torpedo or any of the others but *Dynamo*, because, you'll have us believe, they're the only side that can truly be said to be above team rivalry . . .'

'. . . *representing*, as they do, the secret police, and through them the Soviet state and all her citizens. Yes, Comrade Tomsky, I think we now understand one another perfectly well. Failure to do this will result in us all being pulled up in front of a people's court on charges of attempting to facilitate the creation of a bourgeois sporting elite. As sportsmen there's just a chance that you'd get off with your lives, but for the rest of us failure to comply would mean certain death.'

'Zayets, have you any idea how difficult it is to deliberately lose a game in front of seventy thousand paying spectators, or how hard it's going to be for us to sell the idea to eleven professional athletes . . .'

'Comrade Tomsky, with the stakes being what they are I'm not sure I agree with you. Listen to reason. No one is asking you to do this every week, just enough times for Dynamo to level on points with you and win the league. You can still come second.'

'I don't know, I really don't know,' said Tomsky, shaking his head.

Copic sat where he was, his face oscillating between purple and dark red.

Rykhly coughed nervously and motioned towards the door. 'Perhaps it's best if you go away and think about this today and get used to the idea, so to speak, then, maybe later tonight, Comrade Copic can come back and settle the matter with Zayets . . .'

'An excellent idea, Rykhly. It's obvious that both of you have had quite a lot to take on board for one morning. Far better if me and Igor Ivanovich meet later over a bottle of vodka and discuss the ins and outs of the whole thing man to man.'

'I don't know what difference talking about this will make but I expect it can't be any worse than what we've already endured this morning,' said Tomsky, his black eyes flickering with disgust. 'Do you hear that, boss? You've a cosy one-to-one with Zayets ahead of you.'

Copic looked up at Zayets and closed his eyes.

'I'll take that as a yes, then, Comrade,' said Zayets by way of a conclusion.

'*Yes*,' said Tomsky.

Copic said nothing.

Shkaf, who had watched the whole drama unfold like one who had already been bitten by the snake, got up and patted Copic on the shoulder.

'I tell you something, Igor Ivanovich, they're worse than the landowners, *even worse than the landowners . . .*'

Tomsky buttoned up his jacket and put on his cap. It was hard not to agree. Gently he touched Copic on the back of the head and pointed towards the door.

'It's time to go, boss.'

# Chapter Four

Klimt Grotsky, arch enemy of Copic, regional head of the NKVD and manager of Moscow Dynamo, had been hammering away at Lotya Pantya for fifteen minutes and was already bored. He could usually last longer than this. She had been awake when he started and, at first, he had simply tried to get on with it. It had taken two senseless minutes for him to start thinking of his first wife, a big-breasted Chechen hussy, but this image relied heavily on there being a fat set of tits stacked under his own flabby chest, and Lotya did not possess these. Different naked women flitted back and forth, before his mind's eye settled on the arse of a good friend's wife, but little Lotya's broken yelps were a continual reminder of her presence, destroying the picture of the rump almost at once. Finally, and without willing it, he had pictured himself naked, except for a moist jockstrap, standing in front of a mirror, which was still not enough to relieve the tedium of making love to a woman he could not get through to.

'Thundering fuck, I'll snap your quim in half!' he yelled, knowing at once that it was no use. There was just no way of reaching the smooth plateau of auto-fuck where, he hoped, his body would take over and his mind could give up. For no matter how far he took it, the more he tried to excite himself, the farther removed from his actual sex drive he became.

'Damn you!' he screamed, and smashed the corner of the four-poster bed with his ring-encrusted hand. Lotya lay there, silent and insensible, her tiny white freckled face a puzzle he had no inclination to solve.

'You sterile little tart,' he barked. 'Most women would die for this,' he gestured, slapping his penis against his leg. 'Is it any wonder I'm always fucking other women when this is all I have to come home to, eh? Well, is it, you mute bitch?'

Lotya pulled the sheets up over her ears and turned over on her side.

Grotsky grunted, climbed off the bed and staggered into the adjoining bathroom.

'I should have left you to rot where I found you,' he shouted back at her, his voice less angry now. 'You'd still be taking it up the arse from your brothers and uncles in that stinking hole of a village, wouldn't you? That's right, say nothing and just lie there like a good little peasant girl . . .'

And on it went. Lotya lay there, listening to the man who had changed her life, biting her lip at every foul-mouthed expression addressed to her, yet agreeing with every word. For the truth was that if it weren't for the thickset monster who stood in the bathroom, scratching the mixture of muscle and fat that was his buttocks, Lotya would still have been the sex slave of a large and extended family of Eskimo trappers. Or at least this is what Grotsky thought, because this is what she had told him. In reality she had run away from a poor but loving mother and father, who coddled her as they would any free gift from God. Again and again they impressed on her the need to *save* herself for the right man or task. This went on for so long that she started to wonder what was so important about her that required saving. So when Grotsky had spotted her in the soup queue she had jumped at her chance, fed him a cock-and-bull sob story, and been whisked away to the city as his mistress where, for a while at least, she had enjoyed being spoilt. But as the weeks turned into months, and those parts of herself that existed outside her capacity for excitement caught up with her, she felt a withdrawal occur, both from Grotsky and life in general.

This was why the image of the strange little boy with the red pudding bowl she had spied yesterday had been impossible to get rid of. His face was that of her brother, or of any one of the simple and kind people in her village, a reminder of a purer and lighter world than the one she now lived in. The relentless corruption and evil she had subjected herself to had, to her shame, exhausted her desire for adventure. Now all she wanted to do was to return home.

Grotsky walked back to the bed. 'You've been given the whole lot but you still can't enjoy yourself,' he shouted, tapping his bald head. 'I don't know what the point was in getting you enrolled in that gymnasts' school but it doesn't have any effect on you, nothing does, you just wander around like an inbred corpse. When I think of the hours I've put in trying to make something of you, those long thankless hours, but with no return at all . . .' He hauled up his heavy black jodhpurs. 'Ahhh, go to hell, you're not grateful enough to be worthy of my worry.'

With a lost look in her eyes, Lotya moved to the end of the bed and bent her head over Grotsky's crotch, her cold fingers pulling his jodhpurs back down over his pillar-like thighs. It was the only way she knew of retaining her keeper's favour.

'Better, Lotya, much better . . .' He sighed as the force of a passing Metro train shook the room to its flimsy foundations. 'Much better, you fruity little slut, much better.' ·

Far away Lotya could hear her grandmother calling her to dinner and her brothers playing tag. For the first time in her life she found herself wishing she were still at school. At least there were people to play with there.

Above her Grotsky, blind to everything except his own pleasure, manoeuvred his way in and out of Lotya's mouth with the brute disregard of a delinquent breaking glass. It wasn't so much that he enjoyed watching another human being belittled, it was just that he did not believe that he could trust one until they had been. Curiously this was not a view he had ever thought of testing on himself, but then consistency was not a quality he prized highly. As Chief of Secret Police he had no need to.

'You like that, don't you? You like to choke on my . . .'

'Yes,' said Lotya, removing his member from her mouth, 'yes, I do.'

Grotsky felt his erection sag a little; it was not a question he had asked for the purpose of an answer.

'Well, hurry up and choke on it, then,' he grunted. 'The morning's already half over.'

Sullenly, but with slightly more life in her eyes, Lotya returned to her task, nibbling now like a hungry fish, happy that Grotsky's face was reddening with overwrought frustration.

'God, we'll be here till Christmas if I had to wait for you,' he shouted, checking his watch. 'Clear up in here. I'm off to the shower to finish the job myself.'

Lotya watched Grotsky rush back into the bathroom with mild surprise. Usually he would have used her mouth like a urinal. Might he have changed a little? The thought caused her to smile for the first time that day.

Getting up on the bed, Lotya resumed her place among the cold pile of sheets. A clock struck eleven and the room started to shake again with the thundering roar of the Metro. There was no doubt at all left in her mind now – she would have to take matters into her own hands and leave him. The question was how?

Copic and Tomsky sat side by side in complete silence. Neither had said a word since leaving the battlements of the Red October Leatherworks. This was especially hard for Copic, as countless Spartak fans had identified him since they had climbed aboard the Metro. And yet he had not been able to return even a greeting to any of them.

The meeting they had just attended had confirmed their very worst fears about the Soviet Union, but neither of them knew how to say this to the other. The subject had never been directly broached before. So instead they sat in silence.

'It's just not fair,' said Copic at last, aware at once of how pathetically inadequate this remark was.

'That's the kind of thing I'd expect to hear from Radek,' quipped Tomsky unconvincingly.

Out of the corner of his eye the secret policeman watched them exchange banalities with surprise; as an expert lip reader he could decipher every word they said but he was shocked to find them saying so little. He had at least expected some oaths and curses, but instead both coach and manager resembled nothing so much as disappointed schoolboys. It was at times like this that he wished he had a skill only the best spies in the world could boast of – the power to see into men's minds. If he had possessed this he would doubtlessly have heard the conversation he wanted to hear; one that was full of subversion and resentment towards the authorities. Because this was, in fact, what both men were thinking and feeling.

Copic hated the Party and hated the system; he just did not know that he did. This was partly because he had not always felt this way, but also because, as a lifelong champion of the peasants and the working class, this thought was unthinkable to him. Over the years plenty had happened to challenge the conviction that he was living in the greatest society mankind had ever known: the arrest and persecution of old friends, the detainment and disappearance of his sons, the confiscation of the Bible and prayer book his mother had left him and the loss of many of his most basic freedoms. Unlike many of his contemporaries he had neither the religious faith in the Party nor the armoury of intellectual self-justification required to help him through these trials. He had faced them alone and did the only thing he could do to keep mind and soul intact; he ignored them wherever possible and comp-artmentalised them as anomalies anywhere they were too blatant to ignore. The price he had paid was the loss of his sanity and a constant, unspecified anxiety. Everything he feared, doubted or hated about the system was rigidly blocked off from the rest of his life, thus leaving the bulk of his personality free to be as idiotic as he wished, obsessed with football and other playful interests. The end result was one in which Copic did not know, and did not want to know, his own mind.

Tomsky, on the other hand, hated the Party and knew himself to do so. It was just that he had never told anyone and had restricted his disapproval to the odd sarcastic remark. But these were the types of remarks that made the listener believe that Tomsky was the ultimate insider, a man who could see what the current system's faults were and still back it to the hilt. This was certainly the opinion of the Party bigwigs who had watched Tomsky's progress over the years, acknowledged his cynicism and yet never distinguished it from their own. Tomsky had been careful never to let them, always choosing jobs that had held the promise of disgusting him the least, whether agitating among Negroes in far-off lands, or at home working in the 'soft' industries like sport and leisure. But no matter how innocuous his choice of locale or job, or how hard he kept his head down, the long arm of Party absurdity was always able to catch up with him. Despite their close intimacy, Tomsky and Copic had never discussed matters like this openly, and yet their conversation was full of allusions and insinuations that only someone who had feelings like these would understand. It was a strange situation, but one utterly in keeping with the times.

It was with this in mind that Tomsky decided to risk his life in a single sentence.

'Shkaf's right, they're lying, murderous, pathetic little bastards and I wish every one of them dead.'

Copic's face went white. 'Be careful what you say here.'

'I know every age has to live with its absurdities but, as of today, ours have become too much to bear.'

'Fuck me, Tomsky, this is no place for the Sermon on the Mount, whether people know what you're talking about or not.'

The spy, desperate to see what was going on, tried

to push in between two sailors who, just as desperate to be left alone, pushed him roughly back into his seat and stamped on his toe.

'Come on, Igor Ivanovich,' said Tomsky, grabbing Copic's arm and lifting him out of the train on to the bustling platform, 'we need to talk.'

'We're in a situation where we can't keep lying to one another any more,' said Tomsky, pleased that he was off to such a confident start. 'Our heads have been in the sand too long. Life won't let us keep them there now, it's time to wake up and take hold of . . .'

'All right, all right, this isn't half-time team talk and I'm not some muttonhead, but please, please, lower your voice. We're in enough shit as it is.'

'And we'll be in even more if we don't face up to what's happening to us,' said Tomsky, sure that what was coming next would make hard hearing for Copic. 'It might be dangerous to speak this frankly but it'll be more dangerous if we remain silent and wait for our end like a couple of prunes.'

Taking Copic's hand, he gave it a squeeze and thumped him lightly on the chest. Copic seemed not to notice, his eyes drifting like gulls, along the frozen banks of the Volga and beyond into the bright white distance of the Platsky shipyards. It was difficult to tell whether he was lost in thought or simply stunned.

'I know there's no point in talking too openly or saying too much, we both appreciate that, but I think we've arrived at a place where it's important for our own safety to know where the other's coming from. To do that means taking a few risks of our own and not holding back . . .'

'Okay, okay, none of your psychological horse shit, Tomsky, we've lived too long to pretend we don't know what we're talking about . . .' snapped Copic, back from his daydream.

'That's precisely what I was trying to say . . .'

'No,' said Copic, lifting his hand, 'you've had your say; now hold that tongue of yours and let me have mine. This situation, yes, it *is* a damned daunting one, and I'll be the first to admit it. I've never encountered anything like this in my life before; everything seems to be turned on its head. There's no use pretending anything else. But we'll have to stare it down as it is . . .'

'That's exactly what I was trying to say . . .'

'You see, Tomsky, this is our greatest challenge yet, a real tight corner that calls for real men, one that will separate the iron from the anvil, if you see what I mean.'

Tomsky smiled wryly. Copic was back.

'And you're right, we're probably in danger anyway now so it doesn't pay to hold our noses and tongues and pretend that nothing's happening, because the time for that has already passed. But as I was saying, one thing we don't have a lot of is time – in particular, time for talk, something I know you're a little too fond of – so what I'm saying is we can't afford to stand around psychologising like a pair of Catholic martyrs. We've all got our gripes against the system, who hasn't? It's not perfect and not even the boss would pretend it is. But the important point is to not think about those gripes now. If we did we'd probably go fucking mad and anyway we haven't the time.' Copic stopped for a moment, as if to acknowledge just how terrible, and yet inevitable, those 'gripes' were, before concluding, 'So what I want to hear from you is a plan of bloody action, and I don't mean the kind you can get from my uncle's whorehouse in Irkutsk.'

It was Tomsky's turn to appear dazed.

'Come on, come on, I've already told you time isn't on our side,' urged Copic, confident now that he was on his way to saving the situation.

'It's hard enough to know what the real problem is, let alone any solution.'

Copic nodded impatiently. 'Of course, I could have told you that, but you're the one who was keen to talk openly, so start talking. You'll find me all ears.'

Tomsky smiled slightly, amused at the speed with which Copic could recover from a knock and talk on his feet, irrespective of the raised stakes. 'Right, then, the first thing is that we don't know who we're dealing with yet ... and until we do, we don't know how serious this is, so until we find out we should carry on as if we know nothing, because in the end that's exactly what all this could be. Nothing.'

'Are you trying to say that they might be having us on? Because if it's an elaborate practical joke, then they're playing their parts to perfection.'

'Not exactly. This "idea" of theirs might have origi-
nated in some Party back-stabbing, a union feud, a
grudge against you and me taken to a new level.
Perhaps there's even something in what Zayets said,
or maybe it's just a load of bollocks designed to stop
us getting ideas above our station. Whatever, it can't
be too serious because if it were we'd have been hearing
from the NKVD and not a pawn like Zayets. Besides,
we enjoy considerable protection through our status,
we're not a couple of unknown poets who can be
arrested and bumped off in the middle of the night,
it just wouldn't be credible. We may be a pair of idiots
in their eyes but we enjoy two of the highest profiles in
Russia, and even in a place like this that must count
for something.'

Copic nodded eagerly, impressed that Tomsky's
grasp of the situation appeared to be equal to his
own. He had always thought that people were wrong
about Tomsky, that far from being cynical there was an
essential naivety about him. Now he was not so sure.

'You've made it sound damn simple, I'll grant you
that, but I still don't know . . .'

'That's because confusion's absorbing and answers
aren't – they're direct and simple irrespective of the
path they have to follow. You taught me that.'

Copic continued to nod, sure that he could never
have said such a thing, but pleased to have it attributed
to him.

'Yes, I *know* that, but even so I'm still worried about
where all this trouble comes from. Things seemed to be

going so well for us up until today. This could be any of the things you suggested, but we saw a different side to those men today. Zayets was a complete stranger to me. I've seen that happen with other people before, and once it does things usually start to change for the worse.'

'Perhaps by this evening Zayets'll be ready to tell you what's *really* going on and what he actually wants from us, because there *is* a deal to be struck and it won't have anything to do with the crap we heard earlier today, believe me.'

'And what will you do?'

'I have a source of my own I'll tap later on. So don't worry, it might look bad now, but by tonight we could be looking at a completely different situation. The one thing that really got me, though, is the way Zayets spoke to us earlier, with absolutely no respect for our position or intelligence. For me it demonstrates that he's trying to scare us because he's got nothing real to hit us with. Anyway, by tonight we'll know.'

'And in the meantime you say we should carry on like nothing's happened?'

'Yes, for the moment there's nothing else we can do, short of worrying uselessly.'

This was music to Copic's ears. He gave Tomsky a good-natured pinch on the nose and reached for his pipe. The sun was shining again and he would be wearing his new tracksuit at practice in half an hour.

'I'd better get over to the training ground, then.' He

laughed. 'And you, you have a date with Radek, if I'm not mistaken?'

Tomsky raised an eyebrow. 'Yes, I had forgotten all about him. Back on to the beloved Metro, then,' he said, pointing towards the station entrance.

By the time they had got to the ticket stiles Copic was already signing autographs and boasting that Dynamo were going to catch the fucking of their lives, come the weekend.

Slovo watched the ice-skaters slice the wig into little red shreds.

'I wish you hadn't done that,' said Kasper. 'You may not have liked it but it deserved better than that. My uncle takes a lot of care in making those things.'

'I should have punched those street urchins in the snout,' said Slovo, the taunts of the children still ringing in his ears.

'Nah, they're just kids, not worth it . . . but the wig, you shouldn't have thrown it in, it cost money and . . .'

'Did I really look like a rent boy in it?'

'No, of course not, I've already told you that's just the kids being spiteful. You looked . . . different, that's all. Anyway, so what if the wig didn't work out, you don't look so bad bald, it quite suits you in a way.'

'*Baldy, baldy!*' shouted a porky little newspaper seller.

'At least he can get in and out of the front door in the morning,' Kasper retorted.

'Are are you two sleeping with each other or something?' The ruffian leered.

'I ought to smash your bloody chops in,' screamed Slovo.

'Why don't you come here and say that, you bald cunt?' The youngster laughed, as he raised an elbow and disappeared down a side street.

Dropping his kitbag, Slovo darted across the towpath, over the road, and into the maze of surrounding streets, swearing a terrible vengeance on the boy, should he catch him unrepentant.

Unimpressed, Chief Grotsky watched the little drama unfold from the warmth of his chauffeur-driven *Lil* Limousine. He had been hoping to arrest a Spartak player on a public order offence for some time now, but the battering of a street child would be thrown out of any self-respecting court, even a rigged one. Tapping his driver on the shoulder, he motioned him to drive, away from the slums and their intestinal smells.

The road up to Radek's apartment reminded Tomsky of the one where he had lived in Chicago. Both were very elementary. The only difference was the colour of the men fishing in the open sewers. In Chicago they had been black, whereas in Moscow they were the shade of faded paper.

Tomsky eyed the building warily. There seemed something patently absurd about trying to inspire a striker to play in a game they had just been ordered to throw. Both his hands were trembling, despite being buried deep in his pockets. There was no doubt about it; he was worried about what he had said to Copic. It was impossible to know whether he had been right or not because he had wanted to believe what he was saying too much to trust his own judgement. So long as he could still hear his voice saying those reassuring words there seemed a good chance of them being true. But as he walked in silence, their memory was eroding fast, and along with it the control they had helped to impose on his fear. They were just words but the situation was real. Carefully, and not a little pathetically, Tomsky started to repeat them to himself. It took a full recital before it dawned on him that their power to order reality had, quite suddenly, vanished. They were just sounds now. Sounds invented to comfort Copic, and himself.

In the distance he could see the huge red star of Radio Moscow flashing through the mixture of smoke and fog, its circumference twinkling menacingly like a reminder of all that was bad in the world. He shook his head. What he had said earlier was bullshit. They were in trouble now, real trouble.

Grotsky closed the heavy oak door as hard as he could, forcing his subordinates to jump to attention. Although he did this every day, the routine never ceased to excite him. Next to the sound of a fist breaking a cheekbone, the noise of a slamming door was by far the most satisfying one he knew. Crossing the room, he sat down behind his enormous mahogany desk and looked out of the window and across the square at the Spartak offices.

'The bastard,' he muttered, 'the stupid exhausting bastard.'

'Shall I tell the first team you're ready for them now, Chief?' said Grotsky's team secretary, Babel, a studious-looking young Jew.

Grotsky, ignoring the question, grinned at him like a lecher.

'Babel.'

'Chief?'

'You know why I keep you on here, don't you?'

'Chief?'

'It's because I'm still having fun working out whether you're a monk or a repressed homosexual.'

On account of the cold the skin on Babel's bottom lip was parched, so when he bit down on it it broke, leaving a slight trickle of blood above his chin.

Grotsky noticed it and smiled. 'Because if you're a monk I'll have to kill you, but if you're a faggot, well then, I'd have no choice but to fuck you till you squeaked. So what do you say to that, Jew boy?'

Without blinking Babel replied, 'I am not a faggot, monk or a Jew, sir, I am a communist.'

Grotsky let out a gruff laugh. 'Good answer, Babel, good answer. Tell Popov and Gorfsky I'll be ready to address the team in ten minutes. Cretor, you stay here, we've something to discuss and, unfortunately, I'm going to need your opinion on it.'

Olig Cretor, assistant manager of Moscow Dynamo

and one-time police informant, bowed his head dutifully and clicked his heels. Although he had known Grotsky for nine years previously, and had been his assistant for five more, such displays of formality were still required when in front of subordinates like Babel.

Babel, grateful that he was to be spared any further humiliation, hurried out of the room to convey his message to the team captain and coach.

Grotsky eyed his assistant suspiciously, alert for any chink in the oath of loyalty he would repeatedly force from Cretor on their drunken evenings together.

'So what did you get up to last night?'

'Oh, nothing.' Cretor laughed, his instincts as fast and mendacious as those of an Odessa guttersnipe. 'Just fucked the wife, that's all.'

Grotsky choked loudly and banged the desk with his gold signet ring. 'Just fucking the wife' meant fucking Grotsky's ex-wife, the big-breasted Chechen hussy he had deserted years ago. Grotsky, who had grown bored with her, had originally instigated this arrangement by 'giving' her to Cretor. This had suited his clan-like sensibilities as it had provided an extra dimension to his professional ties with Cretor, and kept his ex-wife within reach too. His pleasure only increased once he realised that Cretor had actually fallen in love with the woman, thus allowing him to subject his assistant to continual and deeply personal taunts regarding his wife's fidelity and sexual prowess. For a while it had seemed like the perfect situation, abusing Cretor's sensitivity during the day, and fucking his wife by night. However, as Cretor, and his new wife, grew closer to one another and even appeared to enjoy being married, Grotsky had felt the situation turn. Cretor had noticed this subtle shift too and had recently taken to boasting about the joys of intercourse within marriage, so much so that Grotsky had started to wonder who was fucking who every time the subject was brought up.

'For the love of God! You think I'm interested in you and your syphilitic Chechen? I had my fist in her arse before you even had a look-in, so there's nothing you can tell me about her that I don't already know.'

'Of course not, Chief, no one was suggesting there was.'

Grotsky scowled darkly, angry to be reminded of the gap between his authority and his power.

'Be careful, Cretor, what I make I can take away and break. Remember that when you're lying in bed sucking the titties of that wife of yours.'

'I will, Chief.'

There was an unpleasant silence, typical of the pauses that characterised the relationship between the two men.

'I suppose you've arranged an agenda today?'

'Of course. Would you like me to tell you what it is?'

'Get on with it.'

'Me and Popov will take training this afternoon so you can meet the Boss for your weekly briefing. The talk this morning will be on the duality of ideology and tactics. Babel has left notes for you on the podium in case you should get . . . stuck. The lads will also expect you to say something about the game against Kiev on Saturday, a stunning victory even if I do say so myself, and of course, a few words about the game against Spartak on . . .'

'I'll handle the last bit, you can do the rest,' interrupted Grotsky, his powers of delegation as strong as ever.

'Of course, Chief. Are we ready to go through, then?' Grotsky's office was adjoined to a lecture theatre in which he would give his morning briefings, once the Dynamo players had received their hour-long political education from Popov, the team 'coach'.

'Wait a minute. Before we go in I'd like your opinion on where those sons of bitches' heads are at the moment.'

'I'm sorry, Chief?'

'Spartak, those bastards at Spartak, who else could I mean?'

'I'm sorry, Chief, I thought you meant our own team.'

'Don't get coy with me, Cretor, just answer the question.'

Cretor shrugged his shoulders. 'They're certainly on a high at the moment. There's no doubt about that . . .'

'But how much have the management to do with it? That's the question we never get to the bottom of, and that's what I need to know. You see, I've been thinking about this a lot recently and my theory is that Copic is a vodka-swilling dinosaur and it's his number two, the psychologist Tomsky, who really puts in the hours. Maybe it's him we should be targeting.'

'Really? From what I hear Tomsky's too busy chasing skirt to do any work and most of the training comes down to their coach, the Catalan Josip Guardiola. Maybe if we had a proper coach instead of a political attaché we'd be in the same position as them, and not wondering what their "secret" is.'

'You may have a point there but that still doesn't explain their way with tactics, formations, motivation and so on. And it's more than them being full time and us part time. Hardly any of our players do any police work now anyway.'

'I know, I know. However you look at it you have to hand it to them, Copic and Tomsky have really got something going between them and that team.'

'Even though man for man our players are at least equal to theirs?'

'Yes, with the exception of five positions . . .'

'Skip the Radek discussion, we've already had enough of it. Get on to the other four you're thinking of.'

'Guardiola himself, probably the most gifted wing-back of his generation, Kasper their goalkeeper, the man's a gorilla, Slovo in midfield, we haven't seen half of what he's capable of yet, and of course Makhno – even at his age you can put him anywhere, even between the posts, and he'd still perform like a detachment of Ukrainian partisans. What's worse is that they're all unpredictable, and not in a sloppy way either, but in the sense that they'll always find a new way of getting behind and among the opposition. With a nucleus like that it's no wonder that Copic and Tomsky have such fun assembling the parts.'

'And we just can't find a way of breaking them down . . .'

'Not for any want of trying, Chief. Last time I instructed our boys to run at them head on, fight for every fifty-fifty and not care if a few of 'em ended up in the san, but the thing with these Spartak boys is they don't mind mixing it with the best of them, which is odd for such a group of players with flair. That's where I think Copic's influence is most felt. Tomsky's there in the wings to understand what makes them tick and then there's Guardiola to thrash out the practical aspects of the programme. At least, that's what our plant tells us, but he isn't the brightest of lads . . .'

'So to beat them we'd have to find some way of physically depriving their team of one or two of those constituent parts. The trouble is we'll make ourselves a laughing stock if we arrest any of them, the important ones anyway, and with the lesser ones it wouldn't make much difference whether we fitted them up or not. It's amazing that the people understand the necessity of foul play in politics but if we try it in sport we risk undermining our credibility . . .'

'I've always said sign a couple of them – obviously not a political like Makhno but one of the younger ones, Slovo perhaps . . .'

'You know, that's the one thing I can't make happen. To be a Dynamo player you have to be a member of the NKVD or the Communist Party. It would be impossible, even with my connections, to fit a Spartak player up like that.'

'But we *are* still a very good team, we shouldn't lose sight of that.'

'I know, Cretor; it's just that they're a better one. Which brings me on to my next question. Do you think there is any way we could beat them in a *fair* game of soccer this weekend?'

Cretor shook his head. 'Not this weekend, no. We will eventually but not this weekend, it's too soon. Still, everything comes to him who waits, and we're patient . . .'

'To those who wait and to those who are *prepared*. We *will* win this weekend, Cretor, and it won't be because we're a better team, though incidentally there *are* those who think we are. The reason we'll win is because we'll be prepared, Cretor, better *prepared*.'

Grotsky smiled mysteriously and broke the ruler he had been playing with in half, a fair substitute in the absence of a slamming door, he thought.

'Right, Chief, *right*.' Cretor nodded, happy that it did not really matter whether he knew what Grotsky was talking about or not. Things would happen just as they always did, and for once it seemed that it was someone else's turn to be fucked over, and not his.

There was a knock on the door. It was Babel – ten

minutes had passed and the team were still waiting for their briefing.

Rising from his chair like a Tartar patriarch, Grotsky glanced slyly at the Spartak buildings on the opposite side of the square and licked his lips. 'You bastard,' he whispered. 'I'll fix you, you bastard.'

# Chapter Five

Unlike most of the tenement blocks Tomsky was familiar with, Radek's did not smell of boiled cabbage, indicative, no doubt, of the relative wealth of its inhabitants. Mr and Mrs Radek had been unhappy with the thought of their boy living in the shared players' accommodation laid on by Spartak. Instead they had spent their nest egg renting a room for him in the palatial Nikolai Gogol building, its wooden structure dating back to the days of Tsar Alexander II.

Spoilt bastard, thought Tomsky, as he ascended the oak staircase leading to the fifteenth-floor love nest that Radek had once shared with Katya Polya. Despite his not having kicked a ball for Spartak in a competitive match since the arrival of Josip Guardiola, Tomsky's natural vanity, and the efforts he made on its behalf, had kept him in good shape. The journey up the steps was therefore accomplished quickly, without any loss of breath or composure. This was unfortunate, as Tomsky had hoped to use the staircase as a buffer zone in which to prepare his speech to Radek. Instead he found himself standing outside Radek's door desperately rehearsing the clichéd reassurances favoured by idiots to comfort those hurt in love.

'Fuck it, trust my instincts,' he muttered, and hammered out the rhythm of a Volga boat song on Radek's knocker.

He waited for a minute. There was no answer. He knocked again, this time more gently than before.

'Radek, it's me, open the door, you soppy bastard.'

There was still no answer.

'Listen, you're not in any trouble, I've come round for a chat, not a bollocking.'

Listening carefully, he could hear a slight thump and the sound of feet shuffling towards the door. A lock was unfastened and the door opened.

Before him stood Radek, clad in his first-team jersey and what appeared to be a kilt. He looked like shit.

'Are you going to let me in?'

Sheepishly, Radek stood to one side, allowing Tomsky to enter the freezing apartment.

'Bloody hell, it's cold in here,' said Tomsky, 'but I don't expect you care about little things like that at the moment, do you?'

Radek turned bright red and Tomsky kicked himself for being sarcastic when he had meant to be kind.

The room was littered, unsurprisingly, with personal artefacts; large Polish quilts hung from the walls, a canoe paddle propped up a pile of home-made cushions and a large photograph of Radek and Katya hung above the bed, as if it were the work of a venerable old master. There was no doubt that the photo reflected a happier time, one that could probably be described, at least by Radek, as golden.

'When was that picture taken?' asked Tomsky.

'In the summer of 1936 when we first arrived in Moscow.'

'You were childhood sweethearts, weren't you?'

'No, I met Katya in a café in Vladivostock. I was seventeen, she was, I think, already eighteen years old by then.'

'The older woman, eh?' said Tomsky, surprised again at his ability to say the wrong thing.

'She was working there as a waitress and . . . and I knew right then that it was wonderful to be noticed by such a beautiful girl.'

Tomsky coughed uncomfortably. 'Yes, she was certainly a very good-looking woman. I think it was something everyone commented on at the time.'

Tomsky had some vague recollection of having said that he would have liked to have given her one, but on meeting her he had revised his opinion. It was obvious that she loved, and would only ever love, Radek, and besides, she was not a person about whom it was easy to be sordid. There was at the very centre of Katya, Tomsky felt, a fresh and utterly delightful naturalness, certainly a powerful quality that he was unaccustomed to seeing in girls from the starvation-hit provinces. Radek had, of course, been besotted, but it had been difficult for anyone else to share his rapture for the simple reason that Katya existed only for Radek and no one else. It was therefore impossible for other men to develop any kind of relationship with her at all. Only once, at the end of a boozy party, had she looked at

Tomsky without her usual protective distrustfulness, and, at that moment, he had been able to understand why Radek loved her as he did. Nevertheless, the moment was an isolated one never to be repeated. Soon after the end of that first season Katya joined the Party and successfully entered its bureaucracy. Her appearances at team events become less and less frequent and Tomsky found her even harder to talk to than before. Instead of her initial impenetrable sweetness, he now saw a colder and stubborn woman, still beautiful but increasingly glacial and withdrawn. It had come as no great surprise to him when the news arrived that she had opted to leave Radek. Despite loving him so much that it made her eyes hurt, she, like many other women of her generation, had chosen control, and perhaps even a career, over love. Which was still preferable to not being able to see the point of either, thought Tomsky, as he stared at the once proud and headstrong Radek.

'Have you anything to drink in here? Something warm, I'm feeling my organs freeze over today . . .'

Tomsky stopped. Not only was Radek not interested, he wasn't even listening. Instead he was balanced on the corner of his bed, head in lap, sobbing fitfully. Tomsky had thought that it would be difficult to feel too sorry for Radek, especially with the problems he and Copic had inherited in the past hour, but he was pleased to find that he was wrong about this. Radek was not, as Copic believed, selfish and indulgent, but hopeless and helpless in the face of emotions that were too strong and unfamiliar for him to understand. Despite himself, Tomsky found that he was experiencing a protectiveness towards Radek; perhaps similar to the kind of thing Katya had once felt towards him. Tomsky sat down. The moment called for something simple. Moving up the bed, Tomsky put an arm around the unfortunate player's shoulder and asked him, somewhat foolishly in the circumstances, what the matter was.

'It's Katya, Eider Ilyich. I can't stop dreaming about her, she comes to me every night like a curse.'

'Ah . . .' said Tomsky, hoping desperately that if he could think of the right thing to say, he might at least be spared the details.

'Only last night I dreamt that she asked me to get something from the shops. It was her voice and her face. When I tried to explain my feelings to her she just became angry, but when I stopped talking she smiled at me, just like she always used to . . . just as I remember her . . . beautiful.'

'Is that right?'

'Then when I wake, she's still in the room, communicating to me through that open window, just as she did many summers ago . . .'

'Communicating through the window? I'm not sure I follow you, Radek.'

'We'd send messages to each other in the evening wind when we were apart, like blowing kisses.'

'Ah, I see, but it's warmer in the summer, isn't it?' said Tomsky, stamping his feet and rubbing his hands to keep them from going numb. 'More, um, preferable to communicate like that when it's not snowing outside, I mean,' he added clumsily.

'How can I live without her, Comrade?' implored Radek, not to be stopped now. 'How can I be led by a part of my life that no longer lives, that part which loved and knew her . . .'

'How do you know that you did?'

Radek stared at Tomsky as though he were stupid. 'I knew her and my knowledge of her was true because she loved me, and now she won't even talk to me . . .'

'Fuck her, Radek, fuck the sour old cow, there can't be a girl in Moscow who doesn't want to leap into the sack with you . . .'

'But kissing the skin of someone you're made for isn't like kissing the skin of someone else.'

'True, true.' Tomsky nodded, amazed that he had never realised how crazy Radek was before, but filled with a strange admiration for him all the same.

'I know I must sound like a weak-willed fool to you, Comrade . . .'

'No, don't apologise,' said Tomsky with a wave of his hand. 'I've got a good idea of what you're talking about, there isn't anybody in the team who hasn't, we've all fallen in love, you know . . . Which reminds me of something. Do you have you any of those Polish cigs your dad sent you knocking around?'

Eagerly, as if to atone for his embarrassment, Radek got up, opened his trunk, and pulled out a carton of cigarettes which he thrust on to Tomsky's lap.

'Here, please keep them.'

'Much obliged, Radek, you're a good lad.'

Tomsky tore open a pack and, after offering Radek a cigarette, lit one himself.

'Have you spoken to your parents about this yet?'

'No, I don't want them to think anything has happened between me and Katya.'

'Is that because you think you might be able to get her back?'

Radek looked at the floor dejectedly. 'Tell me, Comrade, give it to me straight, is she seeing someone else?'

'Not that I know of but I wouldn't draw too much encouragement from that,' said Tomsky.

'Makhno told me she had moved in with an NKVD colonel.'

'She has, but the colonel is a woman. Anyway, that's not important. What she does now is her business, that's what you've got to understand and endure, because she's no longer your responsibility. And look on the bright side; it means you can do whatever *you* want now without her breathing down your neck.'

'But that's where I want her! I don't like it on my own!' snivelled Radek, in streams of tears again. 'I'm sorry, Comrade, I'm sorry for being so weak . . .'

'Oh, come off it, we're all bloody weak,' said Tomsky without conviction, 'weak' being the last thing he actually considered himself to be. 'There isn't one of us who doesn't have trouble holding it together,' he added, reinforcing the lie. 'Anyone can tell you that, and besides, it takes *adequacy* to admit to being pathetic. Most people who are in hell are too scared and dumb to even admit they are. At least you have the honesty to face up to the way you're feeling.'

Radek, whose face was sticky with tears, nodded gratefully. 'Thank you, Comrade, I didn't want you to think that I was abnormal.'

'Abnormal-normal!' snorted Tomsky. 'Don't make me laugh, neither thing exists, not in my experience of life anyway,' he added, disconcerted that he was starting to sound a little like Copic. 'What's normal about me managing a football team or Katya deciding that she'll never speak to you again, you tell me.'

'Nothing, I suppose.'

'Exactly, so forget about normality. The only thing you need to remember is that the world, irrespective of how you may feel about it, is moving along without you. You need to hurry up and join in . . .'

'But how *can* I without my Katya? I'm sorry, Comrade, but you have no idea what it feels like to be in my skin,' sniffled Radek.

'For God's sake, Radek, stop whining! You may think that I don't know anything about the endless hopelessness of being oneself, you may even think that I don't understand what it's like to be in love with someone who doesn't care about you, but for the love of your own dignity stop being so bloody self-indulgent!'

'Comrade, I . . .'

'Listen to me! You've just got to accept that in this

78

life people *do* become dead to one another, and once this happens they cease to be a part of each other's stories. It's fucking awful but there you are, it happens all the time and eventually you come to realise that life just isn't *that* precious . . .' Tomsky paused. What was he talking about? Radek was right. Life *was* that precious.

'But tell me what the point to anything is, then,' said Radek mournfully. 'What's the point of beginning with someone and loving them if one day they'll hate you?'

'I don't know,' Tomsky replied softly. Radek's words seemed to tally with ones he had heard three years earlier from the American he had fallen in love with. His reasons for leaving her had been so practical that he had not given much thought to any of the more abstract questions she had raised. But hearing exactly the same thoughts repeated by Radek brought her words back with an edge they had lacked at the time. Tomsky could feel the first traces of water gather in his eyes. He was in Radek's world now, aware not only of his own pain but the force of all pain in general.

'Look, stop crying, I'll talk to Katya for you.'

Clutching Tomsky's hand, Radek began to tremble furiously. 'Would you really do that for me, Comrade?'

'Yes, but I don't want you to get your hopes up or believe that it'll do any good because it probably won't.'

'I don't care, anything's worth a try,' said Radek, his face animated by the first stirrings of hope.

'Radek, the reason I'm doing this is so you'll realise she's never going to come back to you. Once you do that, you might be able to get on with the rest of your life, something I know you don't give a shit about at the moment. Love only exists when hope allows it space to breathe. By the time I've finished talking to Katya I don't think there'll be much in the way of hope left. It's harsh, but I think it's the only thing that'll bring you through, knowing that there's nothing to look back on or to hope for.'

'But you might find that she's changed her mind . . .'

'Radek. Please.'

It was only when Tomsky had left that Radek realised that the subject of football had barely been touched upon. He had expected a long lecture from Tomsky on how the team was missing his contribution, or on how he was wasting his talent, but it had never come.

Wiping his eyes on a shawl his sister had knitted for him, Radek closed the window and went back to bed, his heart awash in the same unutterable loneliness that had first befallen it when he realised he would never see Katya again, all of one morning ago.

The players moved through the pool of mist on the training ground like early morning phantoms, the afternoon sun blazing but still eclipsed by the grey wall of clouds. All over the pitch shards of melting snow were broken apart like the icing on sponge cakes, crushed under the weight of the advancing players' boots, the savage cold driving even the slowest of them forward.

'Hurry up, you miserable profanity magnets. Caboose! Caboose! For God's sake, Koba, I've seen a stronger instinct for self-preservation in a party of suicidal lemmings than in that forward run! Once again, once again, until you get it right. Now get those legs out, first one side and then the other. No, not both at once, Kasper, this isn't a sex show for the under-tens.'

Hurting with laughter that exacerbated their stitches, the players began to kick their legs out to one side as they ran, mindful of the roving eye and vinegar tongue of their manager, Igor Ivanovich Copic.

'What do you reckon to the new tracksuit, Josip? This stripe's a bit on the flash side, isn't it? Reminds me of the striped trousers I used to wear as a cavalry man. Christ, I used to get a lot of stick off the lads for those!'

Josip Guardiola smiled indulgently and continued, by way of his arms, to direct the players' movements, without answering a question he presumed to be rhetorical.

'I admit, these ones might not be as deep red as those cavalry stripes, but they're still pretty flash, I reckon,' continued Copic, the pleasure rising like steam off his face. 'Still, not everyone can carry off stripes.'

Josip nodded and continued to smile, never once taking his eyes off the players, yet also refraining from giving the impression that this duty was more important to him than Copic's talk of trousers.

Copic liked and respected Guardiola almost as much as he liked and respected Tomsky. In Guardiola he saw a man much like himself, a born survivor who, having traversed the horrors of hell, had come out the other end smiling, albeit somewhat nervously. Not that he would have known this from talking to him, though. There was a silent and solid quality to the Spaniard that led Copic to believe that Guardiola was a man prepared to face up to the consequences of the truth and live with whatever they were, but not one to talk of them lightly. He would have liked to have been certain of this, but perhaps because of the language barrier he encountered a subtle withdrawnness to Guardiola that stopped them from becoming as close as he thought them capable of being. Copic did not object to this too greatly as a certain distance between a manager and his staff was useful, and in any case he had seen what closing this gap had achieved in the case of Tomsky – the man had become insolent, bone idle and bloody cheeky. Which was precisely why Guardiola had had to be drafted in, not only to supplement Tomsky's frequent sabbaticals from the training ground but, more importantly, to teach the players some technical know-how.

'What did you make of Dynamo's performance against Kiev on Saturday?' asked Copic. He had already had this conversation with Josip and Tomsky twice that week, but the sound of words acted as a comfort to him, especially as he was keen to keep his own darker thoughts at bay.

'Not much,' replied Josip, trying to think of something new to say on the subject. 'They got the away result they needed, the two-nil win, but they played like a delivery of robots with hinges for joints. They ground it out like everything else they do.'

'Exactly what I think. There's no passion in that team, no real firefighters . . .'

Josip Guardiola nodded solemnly, the silvery snow-flakes blowing across his face like ocean spray. 'It's always the same with them,' he added, knowing that he was coming to the part of his analysis that Copic liked best. 'They start with that "we're here to play" attitude and then retreat into a watertight phalanx the minute they lose the ball. After that it's hard for a team to prise them open. They let you keep plenty of possession but never give you a clear-cut scoring chance . . .'

'That works against most teams but not when we play them . . .'

'Of course, because against us they throw it all away the minute they try to go forward and counter-attack. They don't like playing against teams that play their football in the severe style; they can't allow for it, it confuses them. That's the thing with Cretor – his whole method is based on what teams have done before and so he bases the whole game plan on them doing the same thing again. He's like what Tomsky calls a reductive . . . I'm sorry, what's the word in Russian?'

'An inductive empiricist, like in the training manual, but don't get hung up about pronunciation. Go on.'

'Yes, exactly like in the training manual. Grotsky doesn't really know anything about football, for him it's just another thing he wants to be the best at, that's why he trusts the manuals and he trusts Cretor. And that's why he fears us. You hear them boast about how they have discovered 'rational football' but they don't realise that 'reason' is just another attitude towards the game. *Clarity* is the true method . . .'

'Reason is an attitude, clarity a method.' Copic laughed. 'You haven't been talking to that gasser Tomsky about this, have you?'

'I have, as it happens. He's an interesting guy. We meet sometimes after practice to talk about football, but not just the game, other things too. He was the first Russian to show me around town . . .'

'That's because he's after that big-breasted strumpet Muerta,' interrupted Copic, jealous that Tomsky and Josip should have joined forces in this way without consulting him first. 'And anyway, I was the first person to attack "rational football" in *Pravda,* not that Johnny-come-lately Tomsky. I'll refer you to my article if you like . . .'

Josip smiled politely. 'I've read one of your articles actually, one you wrote a couple of years ago when Spartak came to play the Basques in Spain.'

'Bloody hell!' exclaimed Copic. 'Which one was that?'

'It was on Makhno's ability to anticipate the game, a very poetic article if I remember rightly. In it you wrote that the use of the cine-camera replay had changed the way you thought about goals and that you could see them before they had happened, the replay moment suddenly becoming the property of fate.'

'Oh, yes! One of my more purple moments but a bloody good piece all the same!'

'It was certainly that. I remember all the papers in the Republican zone dubbed you the famous Russian "football theorist".'

Copic raised an eyebrow proudly and stroked his stubble with interest. The article had been cobbled together by Tomsky for an after-dinner speech in the Bilbao Institute of Technology. Copic had refused to read it at first on account of not understanding what it meant, but had relented when Tomsky had promised to omit the footnotes.

'Yes, I remember the Basques showed us their film footage of the game, it was absolutely remarkable, much less fragmentary and far more of a spectacle than standing on the sidelines screaming your arse off. I believe they brought those cameras and most of the footage over with them when they were evacuated, but those bastards at Dynamo have hogged the whole lot to themselves. A typical abuse of their position but not in the slightest bit surprising. I . . .'

Copic stopped. He did not want to be talking about Dynamo because he did not want to be thinking about them. That had been the whole purpose of the conversation, to forget and to enjoy, rather than to worry and sweat. What he needed to be doing was carrying on as normal. Patting Josip on the shoulder, he turned his attention to the freezing cluster of players huddled in a pack on the touchline. 'Holy crap, Slovo, how the fuck did you get those nicks in your face and what the hell have you done to your hair? Christ, deaf kid, you're a worry to me, you really are. You're meant to stop balls, not wear them on your head. Here – catch!'

The ball flew straight through the air, landing in a snow shower by Slovo's feet. Three other players leapt on him and a tussle ensued, reminiscent of children fighting over marbles on a street corner.

'That's my boys.' Copic sighed contentedly. 'That's my boys.'

There was something about the Felix Dzerzhinsky Collective dining hall that encouraged one to feel sorry for oneself, Tomsky decided, as he poured the scalding tea into a saucer and then back into the cup. Although this was the officially designated space for Spartak and Dynamo members to meet and eat together, the hall usually remained empty during the day and rigidly segregated at night. Outside of mealtimes it was an odd assortment of old men, lonely refugees and relatives of the disappeared who gathered here, normally alone, to exaggerate and confirm their isolation in front of fellow sufferers. It was for this reason that Tomsky came here, both to meet himself and to be left alone by others, safe in the knowledge that few people would put themselves through the torture of reaching him in a place like this. One man who would, however, was Guy Hubbard, serial pederast and Moscow correspondent for the London *Times*.

'What's the gossip, Tomsky, old fruit?' hissed Hubbard, as he walked over to the table, his six foot six inches minimised by his near-theatrical stoop. 'Mind if I park my bum over here? Ah, that's better. I don't know how any of you get used to the cold, I really don't. So where was I? Gossip, wasn't it?'

'Actually, that's why I asked to see you, Guy. I thought you might have heard something that might help me . . .' Tomsky hesitated. He was loath to ask Hubbard for information, let alone admit that he was in a position where he really needed it. But he had no choice. Hubbard was the best contact he, or anyone else in Moscow, had.

'Information!' Hubbard laughed as if this were the first time he had encountered the idea. 'How wonderful! How wonderful that an intensely serious man like yourself needs to ask a carefree old gal like me for information!'

'Don't over-egg the omelette, Hubbard . . .'

'Oh, I intend to, old boy, I really intend to. It's not every day an opportunity to have you at my mercy comes along!'

Tomsky pulled off his cap and ran his hands through his cropped black hair. 'Please, Hubbard, be more discreet. We could be in danger if the wrong people find out about this meeting.'

'Oh, goody!' squealed Hubbard. 'I love it when things get dangerous in this ghastly little Soviet system of yours!'

Kicking Hubbard under the table, Tomsky indicated a nearby table where a known secret police informant had just sat down. Winking conspiratorially, Hubbard narrowed his lips and whispered, 'Well, you'd better let me have it, then, old boy, and all at once, mind. I don't want any holding back for the sake of form.'

Speaking quietly, Tomsky began to outline the events of that morning, playing down his own involvement for fear of what it could later become, first in Hubbard's mind, and later through his overactive mouth. It was a difficult balancing act, on the one hand feeding Hubbard enough information to provoke a response and maintain his interest, but on the other leaving him with no insight into what he and Copic actually thought about the situation, this caution being of the utmost importance as Tomsky had learnt to his cost the dangers of being open about oneself with Hubbard.

Hubbard, for his part, moved his head from side to side like a conductor listening to a gentle and faintly soothing symphony, his ashy white hair and handlebar moustache disguising the fact that he was actually a year younger than Tomsky and, prior to his 'corruption' in Russia, once considered the leading light of the Communist Party of Great Britain. Unlike many of his more conscientious comrades Hubbard had realised that a closed and paranoid system leant as heavily on gossip and intrigue as it did on its police apparatus and five-year plans. It had not taken him long to cast himself as an invaluable go-between, an alcohol-sodden carrier pigeon who could be relied on to shuttle rumours back from his friends in Moscow to his masters in London. Tomsky had been one of the first Russians he had befriended, but their friendship had, to say the least, failed to live up to its initial promise. Both, in their own way, had let the other down – Hubbard's sympathy for the communist regime alienated Tomsky, and Tomsky's exaggerated hetero-sexuality irritated Hubbard.

'Fascinating, Tomsky, absolutely fascinating. Nothing I don't know already, of course, but always fascinating to hear it from the horse's mouth, there being no substitute for personal experience and all that, don't you think, what?'

'So what can you add to it? How much danger are we really in?'

'Well, they've got a point, haven't they?'

'What are you talking about?'

'Running around winning everything and not sharing the credit with anyone else, not very fair, is it? I think there's certainly something to be said for getting your wings clipped a little, just enough for you to realise that if it weren't for this little socialist experiment of Uncle Joe's you, and the rest of your happy little team, would probably still be planting potatoes on the banks of the merry Volga. As it is, agricultural output is at an all-time high and you and that mad Slav manage a football team. What I'm saying is you have to take the rough with the smooth, the good with the bad and the fair with the unfair. Look at the facts. You are now living in a country with tractors, aeroplanes and near-universal literacy, so is losing a game of football such a high price to pay for all your creature comforts, you precious little dear?'

'Near-universal literacy my arse . . .'

'Don't quibble over the details, Tomsky, that's not the point. I'm asking you to think in terms of the broad facts . . .'

'Bullshit, Hubbard, shameless bullshit, and you know it. I asked you for information, not for the history of the USSR as told by an Oxfridge-educated faggot.'

'Ox*bridge*, dear boy, and in any case you wilfully miss the point. I'm only giving in to a lifetime's weakness for playing devil's advocate . . .'

'The Devil doesn't need an advocate, Hubbard. Not in my country, anyway.'

'How very dark and wonderful of you to say so! You know, Tomsky, you may have your problems but it really wouldn't do you any harm to engage in, how should I put it, a certain lightness of spirit every now and then.'

Slowly the number of people trickling into the dining hall was increasing, the kitchen staff hurriedly packing away the bread cakes while teams of cooks wheeled in steaming vats of hot gruel. An oversized gong was banged twice and a hoarse old voice shouted, 'Dinnertime.' One by one the afternoon crowd folded their papers and crept towards the exits, keen to avoid the oncoming swarm of humanity that was the evening rush.

'Listen to me, Guy, this could be serious, it might even be a question of life or death for me. You know as well as I do that today's heroes are often tomorrow's camp fodder, and none of us are any the wiser until we hear that knock on the door in the night. I might be worrying needlessly or I could have entered the last week of my life, I simply don't know. But if you do know anything that could help, please just tell me now.'

Hubbard stroked his cheeks and purred coyly, twisting his whiskers into little curls. Tomsky could smell the mixture of gin and chocolate on his breath, tainted by the sourness of old tobacco. Never before had he so wanted to punch Hubbard in the face, and never had this desire seemed so just.

'I'll tell you what, Tomsky; I'll give you what you want on the following condition. Set me up with that plucky little Hungarian midfielder of yours, you know the one I mean . . .'

'Slovo?'

'Yes, that's him. Stocky little legs and a nice brick-layer's arse.'

Tomsky shook his head. The habit of treating Moscow as a giant male brothel may have been one of the things that gave Russia its special appeal for Hubbard, but despite the blind eye turned by the Party towards its leading British propagandist, Hubbard was still in danger of understimating the individual Russian's conservatism regarding buggery.

'Hubbard, I warn you, try and fuck him by all means, but he'll have killed you before the blood reaches your dick. This isn't one of your punting pals in England we're talking about here . . .'

'That, my earnest friend, is a risk I welcome and am willing to take.'

'Be my guest.' Tomsky laughed. 'Be my bloody guest!'
'Here you are,' he went on, scribbling down Slovo's
home address on a napkin. 'But don't tell me you
weren't warned.'

'See how handsome you are when you smile.' Hubbard
winked as he greedily pocketed the marked tissue and
looked over his shoulder at the police informer. 'Now,
as for your problem, it's both better and worse than you
think. Better for you because as far as I know the boss
thinks the whole thing is ridiculous and is so amused
by it that he won't commit himself one way or the
other, but worse in that Grotsky is doing everything
in his power to fuck you over.'

'So nothing's written in the sand yet.'

'Not yet. They say that the Boss has trouble believing
that a game could matter so much to his secret police
chief and that his natural tendency to enjoy toying with
people's lives, allied to his natural perversity, actually
makes him rather well disposed to you. However, you
don't need to be told how dangerous Grotsky is, even
when acting alone, so I shouldn't start getting cocky
yet, if I were you.'

'And that's it?'

'Basically, yes.'

'Tomsky!' shouted a figure from the other side of
the hall.

Tomsky stood up and waved back. It was Makhno
and a group of youth team players. They were followed
into the hall by the snarling figure of Olig Cretor and
Ivan Drago, centre forward for Moscow Dynamo.

'I think I'd better go now,' observed Hubbard, 'or at least, it would be in our mutual interests for me to do so.'

'I agree,' said Tomsky. 'You can leave through the kitchens if you like.'

'Very thoughtful of you, old man, very thoughtful,' replied Hubbard, picking up his otter-skin hat. 'See you soon, eh?'

'Yes, see you soon,' said Tomsky with relief. It was no secret that Hubbard felt uncomfortable in the company of men, or more than one man he was not on intimate terms with, and consequently Tomsky felt awkward in Hubbard's company when with other men. It was a situation neither man discussed, but both happily bowed before its logic whenever necessary.

'That was Hubbard, wasn't it?' said Makhno, approaching the table with enough food for four men.

'Yes.'

'Well, you must have your reasons.'

It had been a long time since Tomsky had felt the need to 'explain' Hubbard, and it wasn't something he felt compelled to do now.

'I hate the cunt,' said Makhno.

'He's strange, by our standards, but I hear that in parts of England people like him are found everywhere.' Tomsky blushed slightly. It was a pitiful defence.

'Nonsense, he's a parasitic jackal, the worst type of peripheral scum, and anyway, he's a foreigner. The secret police could pick you up for just talking to him.'

'And what did he do to you? Goose your wife?'

Tomsky laughed, surprised by Makhno's vehemence.

'I know his type, that's all. They're out for whatever they can get.'

'He has his faults but you're wrong, he's not that sort of man . . .'

'Have you had a chance to talk to Radek yet?' interrupted Kasper, who had just seated himself to Tomsky's right.

'Yes.'

'And how is he?'

'I don't know whether he'll be playing on Saturday, if that's what you mean.'

'No, of course it isn't, I want to know how the poor kid is. He must still be in a lot of pain. It always takes a few days to snap out of the shock of a relationship ending, before the real horror sets in.'

'There's too much of the "poor kid" and not enough of a boot up his arse, if you ask me,' snorted Makhno. 'What's a broken heart next to typhus or having your legs shot off?'

'Probably the next worst thing for some people,' said Kasper. 'So how's he doing, Tomsky?'

'Miserable but salvageable, so long as he's spared from the Makhnos of this world for another day.'

Makhno spat out a mushroom, his face bristling with amusement, and wiped his mouth across his sleeve. 'I like the kid, Tomsky, but he's soft and he talks too much. You mean well but you're wasting your time. Leave him to me and you'd see some results, mark my words.'

'Not every horse likes to be whipped, Makhno. I know I'd have preferred someone to understand me before kicking me around the park when I was a kid.'

'You enjoy your work too much, Tomsky.' Makhno smiled. 'Nothing wrong with that, I suppose, but you shouldn't close your mind to other methods. As my mother used to say, there's more than one way to mount a cat, and more than one way to mend a broken heart. I favour vodka, a good punch in the stomach and plenty of exercise, whereas you like to talk.' Makhno shrugged his shoulders. 'Talking is good but only after the problem is solved. The right way, especially with the young men, is to *do* things. Understanding one's motivation is a middle-aged luxury. Good for the older ones like you and me but too much for a young colt like Radek.'

Makhno burped loudly and, using his knife like a spoon and his fork like a hand, shovelled another pile of burnt cabbage into his mouth.

'Typical.' Kasper laughed. 'The great master of human psychology speaks!'

The contrast between Makhno's gravely worded Ukrainian dialect and Kasper's sonorous Byelorussian tones could not have been greater, yet in the noise of the dining hall both were lost in the prevailing din. Tomsky smiled. In a minute communication between all neighbours would be transferred to sign language and guesswork.

'Radek's a fine lad, and it's a good thing the world's

moved on far enough to reject your rough-house remedies, Makhno . . .'

Out of the corner of his eye Tomsky could see the bobbing figure of Muerta Astro coming into the dining hall, her tray pressed against her chest like a stack of schoolbooks. Touching Kasper's hand lightly, he said, 'Do me a favour, Kasper. Warn Slovo to expect a call from the Englishman Hubbard . . .'

'Call? What do you mean?'

'I'll explain later when I've more time. I've got to rush. See you lads later.'

'What's all that about?' Kasper asked, turning to his sunken-cheeked Ukrainian friend, who, despite his enormous appetite, never put on weight.

'Lots of different things,' said Makhno, chewing his cabbage as a horse would hay. 'Lots of different things, I should think.'


Seeing Tomsky get up so quickly had taken Muerta by surprise, even though she had come to the dining hall with the express intention of flouncing past his table. The suddenness of his movement threw her, and she turned and fled out of the hall as fast as she could, rushing through the open forecourt and into the pink and blue flames of the late afternoon sky. Her heart was thundering in and out of time and, to her embarrassment, she was giggling like a shaken schoolgirl. Unable to stop herself now, and despite the fact that she thought her face looked fat when she laughed, floods of laughter poured through her like secrets aired for the first time, on and on until her ears rang and her neck felt numb. Perhaps this is why new lovers never know what to say to each other, Muerta thought, not through fear of appearing stupid in the eyes of the other but because of the embarrassing obviousness of mutual attraction.

Tomsky came to a halt a few feet away from her, his face showing signs of breathlessness and con- fusion. Hesitantly, and controlling her laughter, Muerta walked towards him, sure that if she did not stop in time her hands would be all over his face.

'You intrigue me,' she said.

Tomsky said nothing, perhaps hoping in this way to remain intriguing. Instead he stared at the dark red contours of her mouth and took the gloves off her hands.

'And you make my teeth tingle!' she rasped, her tongue hissing between her teeth in a way that reminded Tomsky, unfortunately, of Guy Hubbard's laugh. Ruthlessly he banished the thought and squeezed her hand. She laughed again, this time, to his relief, looking nothing like Hubbard.

'My teeth tingle,' she almost whispered.

'Good,' he said, and leant forward to kiss her, their backs bent together like those of ice-skaters losing their footing in the fading afternoon light.

Back in the dining hall, Makhno pushed away his plate and folded his arms. Opposite him sat Josip Guardiola, staring into his food nervously, his face a distorted sequence of frowns. Either side of them young players greedily stole food from each other's plates, pushing and banging their tables like medieval banqueters. On the Dynamo side of the hall the young Jew, Babel, climbed on to a bench and announced that it was Ivan Drago's birthday. The Dynamo players welcomed the news by rattling their cutlery and cheering, the Spartak players by jeering and whistling catcalls. Standing up in the midst of it all, Olig Cretor began to sing 'Happy Birthday' to the tune of 'The Red Flag'.

'Scum,' said Makhno quietly.

Josip Guardiola coughed uncomfortably and quickly jerked his head back to indicate he agreed. Just next to him Slovo was making faces into his soup in the hope that it would make his hair grow back more quickly. Maybe by Christmas it would reach his nose again.

'I trust the language barrier didn't hinder your appreciation of our political get-together the other night,' said Makhno to Josip.

Josip squirmed uncomfortably and looked around to make sure they were out of earshot. 'No, I understand Russian pretty well, and speak it pretty good too . . . unless you're all humouring me.'

'Not at all. I think you and Miss Astro have shown great aptitude in that area.'

'We had to.'

'Of course you did. No, what I meant to say was did you find the language of the meeting to your liking?'

Josip made a circling motion with his hand, which he hoped would signify nothing.

'Come on, Josip, I'm not some secret policeman trying to sound you out. Talk to me.'

Behind them Augustus Koba, who had been fiddling with his food nervously, stood up and followed a party of NKVD men out through the door, his legs shaking like straws.

'Tomorrow the Dynamo players are holding a big birthday party for Drago at their club. I heard that some of our boys are organising a party in retaliation over at Radek's place as a surprise to cheer him up. We could talk there, if we must.'

'That would be a good idea,' Makhno replied, rolling a cigarette and staring coldly in the direction of the departing Koba, 'a very good idea.'

# Chapter Six

The freezing sleet had been falling since nightfall and the melting snow under Copic's feet crunched like rotten apples. Pulling out the crumpled piece of paper from his pocket, Copic held it under the dim glow of the street lamp and double-checked the address. To his amazement he found that he had not been wrong, Zayets really *had* moved from his old lodgings to the newly built Kirov ranch complex. Rather than the towering concrete abortion of old, Zayets' new house was one of a series of mock North American beach huts, reserved for NKVD men and communist middle management. Copic grimaced; this was not the Zayets he knew of old.

Zayets flung open his front door with an enthusiasm that suggested the events of that morning were an irritating and far-off memory concerning someone else.

'Come in and get out of the cold, Igor Ivanovich. Natalia, fetch our guest some vodka, he must be absolutely parched,' he shouted, as if for a hidden audience.

'Well, to tell you the truth I am. It hasn't been the easiest of days for me, Grishka, not by a long way.'

Zayets put a finger across his mouth and whispered, 'Please, not yet, wait until Natalia and the children are out of earshot. There is much to discuss but not now.'

Copic's face paled considerably, and some of his earlier fear returned to him. This was the trouble, he reflected, with allowing Tomsky to talk him out of his worry; the payback was always bound to be vicious.

Zayets' wife returned with a tray bearing two bottles of vodka and a little milk. Zayets slapped her backside good-heartedly and made some reference to their son, who was progressing through the aeronautics school with the aim of becoming a pilot. Copic swallowed his drink down in one go and Zayets apologised at once, the fate of Copic's sons being something of a sore spot.

'But your daughters, they must be doing well,' said Natalia.

'Yes,' answered Copic. 'Vera and Dunia are still at the navy academy in Leningrad. I thought after their mother's death it would be the best place for them. There was no sense in them staying in the flat with all those painful memories just to keep a sick old bear like me company.'

'You know, the way you handled those girls and then picked yourself up and carried on after Lara's death is extraordinary, Igor Ivanovich. I never knew a man could be so strong.'

'That's Igor Ivanovich Copic for you, Natalia, a giant

among giants. You could throw him into a hurricane and he'd still come out laughing, eh, Copic? You'd still come out laughing, wouldn't you?'

Copic smiled, embarrassed. He had never stopped to analyse his powers of survival before – life was just something you got on with, good when you knew what you were doing and awful when you did not.

'I'll leave you both to talk,' said Natalia and, grinning indulgently, she left the two men in the narrow hallway that led to Zayets' study.

Zayets sighed and, taking Copic by the arm, said, 'I suppose you're wondering how we got all this?'

'I must admit, the thought had crossed my mind.'

'Carrot, Igor Ivanovich, bloody carrot, and I for one was too stupid to see the bloody stick coming. I know it looks grand enough but I could just as easily be living at the bottom of an arsenic well for the good it's doing me.'

'Why did you accept?'

'What! And accept a place in the gulag or in front of a firing squad instead! You know better than that, Copic. When they say jump, you jump.' Zayets groaned and rubbed the side of his hip. Since the end of the Civil War he had carried the fragmented parts of a shell along one side of his body. 'Yes, it doesn't matter what we'd be doing in an ideal world, because in this one we'll do exactly what the Party tells us and then thank it for the privilege. And don't ask me whether that's right or wrong because I've already said enough to earn a tenner in the camps as it is.'

'I had noticed that your tone has changed a bit since this morning. Is there some reason for that?'

'That was this morning, Igor Ivanovich,' grunted Zayets, 'a show that had to be put on, I'm afraid. The factories are full of spies and our offices have been watched for weeks. Whatever I said there was strictly for the Communist Party copy book and can be disregarded as such. I would have told you but I had to keep our encounter realistic enough for the authorities to think it wasn't staged. Believe me, though, what I have to tell you within these four walls is not a whole lot better than what you heard earlier.' Zayets drained his glass. 'A refill?'

'Good idea.'

Copic scratched his nose and quietly let off a fart. 'The stuff you said this morning about the team, can it really be as important to them as all that?' he asked with a flourish, determined to influence the spirit of things.

'It is for that bastard Grotsky, that's for sure. If everything else produces the results he requires, why shouldn't football?'

'And I thought it was just madmen like us who were petty enough to care about the game . . .'

'Ha! Not by a long way. What we're talking about here is the most important, and best-attended, spectator sport in the Soviet Union. Could you imagine as many people gathering in one place for any other kind of non-Party activity? Of course not, so how long did you think it would take before they finally caught up with you? Believe me, if you carried on as you do in any other area of life you'd already be dead by now, and what's more you aren't even the worst. There's Tomsky to consider, the anarchist Makhno, the Spanish Trotskyite Guardiola, to say nothing of the religious lunatic Kasper . . .'

'All right, all right, I know some of the lads are a little . . . strange, but you've got to keep some perspective . . .'

'Perspective! Listen, Copic, what I'm trying to tell you is that there are voices in the NKVD who say that your football club is a front organisation for subversives who just happen to play a little soccer on the side.'

'But you *know* that's bollocks. It's just that Grotsky and the rest of those pricks at Dynamo are jealous that we field a better football team than them. And why anyone higher than him should care about our team, with everything that's kicking off in Europe at the moment . . .'

'Which has got *nothing* to do with us. Don't you see that they don't give a tinker's cuss about things like that . . .'

'You're losing me here, Zayets . . .'

'All right, Grotsky's jealous, and perhaps that is why he has such a hive in his bonnet about Spartak, but even if he weren't you'd still be up to your neck in shit. It worries me that you don't see it, and forget any talk about our leaders caring about what's happening in Europe. They're peasant lads, Europe doesn't exist for them, only football and these damned five-year plans . . . but you don't see it, do you? The night classes you attended with those European teachers must have scrambled your judgement when it comes to your fellow countrymen. We're Russians, Copic, remember that.'

'So we're Russians, then, well done for us. But what else is there for me to see?'

'Where would you like me to start, Copic?'

Copic shrugged his shoulders and pulled his stomach in. The last thing he wanted was a repeat performance of the morning's lecture, but this seemed to be exactly what he had let himself in for.

'For Grotsky and the authorities the whole game of football, and your team in particular . . .'

'*Our* team,' interrupted Copic.

'Oh, grow up, Igor Ivanovich. Football, for them, is coming to resemble the feared "second life", one that stands outside Party regulations and control. Of course, you can say they have a football team of their own, but look at the facts. On the one hand you have Dynamo, and what have you got with them? Long-ball rationalism and a technical game – they're the prefects, in other words – and on the other hand there's Spartak, improvisation, precision passing, a box of tricks every game – basically the goodies by any other name. You don't have to be some romantic intellectual to see it in those terms either. The people are like a swarm of flies with a shared sense of smell, and they can smell it on you, Copic, they can smell it. Take the occasion with that Basque team. They came over here and thrashed

Dynamo over two legs – your boys play them and nearly ninety thousand watched you take 'em apart six-two. There were old men crying on the streets, I tell you.'

'And this is why you want us to throw the game on Saturday.'

'Yes! I want you to do something yourself before you force the authorities to play their own hand.'

Copic sank his drink and glanced out of the window. The wind had picked up and the sleet was turning to snow again. He would probably freeze on the walk back to the Metro, if it was still running.

Frantically Zayets grabbed a piece of paper from the worktop. 'Here, listen to this, a speech the boss made at the start of the season that was sent to all of us union chiefs. 'Sport exists for utilitarian purposes, to promote health and hygiene, defence, labour, productivity, integration of a multinational population into a unified state, international recognition, prestige and nation-building.' Nowhere does he mention a pair of clowns managing a team of over-paid pretty boys. Of course, it wouldn't matter if you were booed off the pitch every time you played or lost ten times a season, but the fact is that you're not. They love you out there and you're abusing that love. Sport should be for the state and for the people, not dilettantes, talented enthusiasts and underclass scum.'

Zayets loosened his collar and undid his top button. He had thrown everything he had at Copic, made his point and probably said more than he had intended, something that Copic's thick skin and head necessitated. But for all that, it still did not look as if he had made contact.

Copic looked up at him and smiled warmly. 'You know, I never thought there was that much to it.'

'They'll only compete with you so long, Igor Ivanovich,' said Zayets, the tiredness evident in his voice. 'They've already tried to meet you on your own terms by fielding their team against yours. Once they realise that it isn't working they'll resort to their usual methods. The ones they used on the Whites, the Mensheviks, the Social Revolutionaries and even your sons . . .'

Zayets stopped talking. He had crossed the line and he knew it.

Copic, his face free of any rancour, nodded slowly, to acknowledge that he'd finally grasped the point.

'So what have they said they'll do to you if . . . I don't listen?'

'Take this place, for starters, and then rehouse us in a camp somewhere in Samara. For the past week they've been telephoning us with threats, dropping hints to our children on their way home from school, notes under the door, you know the type of thing. I daren't talk about it at the office because I know they've got to Rykhly too. I can see it in his little piggy eyes. Perhaps he's even been offered a separate deal in case I fail to come through with the goods, who knows?'

'What about Shkaf?'

'Shkaf is already as good as dead. That's not your fault. You saw how he was this morning, he's stopped acting, completely given up on the game. They gave his cooperative notice of the new deadlines. He turned them down flat, said he'd had enough of living in a sick fantasy, the deadlines were impossible and he wasn't going to pretend otherwise, let alone break anyone else's back trying to meet them. I was surprised he showed this morning. I certainly don't expect to see him tomorrow.'

Copic got up, crossed the room and poured himself another vodka, filling the glass to the brim.

'And what have you heard about us, me and Tomsky? Are we to go the same way as Shkaf, or have they something else in store for us?'

'Almost certainly, if you will it so. What you've got to understand is that unlike almost everyone else in this country your fate is in your own hands. I'd die to be in your position and actually have a choice. As it is I'm trying to beg you to save your own damned life, and mine too, more's the pity.'

Copic tipped his glass over like an eggcup, downing the contents in one. He had always thought of Zayets as a man with one eye on his next move, an ambitious grafter who had worked his way up and was entitled to his comforts, despite the somewhat unsavoury way he had collected them. This new Zayets, a cross between a party rulebook and a desperate old woman, was making him decidedly queasy.

'You've given me a lot to chew over, Grishka, a lot to chew over. Rest assured whatever decision I come to will be one fully informed by the facts as you've explained them. I can say no more than that for the moment.'

'What do you mean, "whatever decision"? There is only *one* decision you can come to. I thought I'd explained that to you.'

'You have, Grishka. And that, almost certainly, will be the one I'll take.'

'*Almost certainly*?' echoed Zayets, his face purple with disbelief.

'Yes,' said Copic, his expression as innocent as that of a Labrador unable to identify its own excrement.

Zayets shook his head and turned his back, the smile on his face a terse cross between pity and superiority. 'Remember, it's not just your own bed you're making, Copic, it's mine and Natalia's as well. Remember that when you make your decision. And your team too, think of them if you will.'

'Don't worry, I will,' said Copic, pushing his glass across the tray in a figure of eight. 'I wouldn't mind another vodka if you're offering,' he added hopefully, eyeing the second bottle with a twinkle in his eye.

Zayets snorted and poured out another measure; the smallest so far, thought Copic, as he accepted the glass with an open smile.

Natalia joined her husband in the study and helped herself to a drink. Zayets' friendship with Copic had always worried her. Although she liked Copic, or had at least for the first few years of their acquaintance, there was an elementary and untutored wildness about him that she also recoiled from and resented. The last place she wished to encounter this quality was in her own house or, worse, in her husband's eyes.

'The trouble with that man is that he can't tell the difference between being tactful and telling a lie. That's why he can't do either, to his cost and to ours.'

'I know, Grishka, it makes me mad that it's our lives and livelihoods, and not his, that hang in the balance. I wish I could do something to help you, but if he won't listen to you he's hardly likely to pay any heed to me.'

Zayets looked up at his wife admiringly; it did not surprise him that she had been eavesdropping. He would probably have done the same thing in her place. They were well matched like that, he reflected.

'So what do you think he'll do now?'

'What, Copic? You expect me to be able to predict the thoughts and whims of that maniac? I wish I could, but, if I'm to be honest, he could do anything next. Since his sons were taken away from him he's become dangerous. Before then he fancied himself as something of a Renaissance man, but since then he's become a drunken idiot. Even the much-vaunted vocabulary he worked so hard on has disappeared – these days he's gone back to sounding like the St Petersburg guttersnipe he probably always was. The trouble is that the only thing he lives for now is that football team, which is why it's impossible to predict his next move; they're everything to him.'

Natalia smiled weakly, tiny beads of sweat collecting around the edges of her hairline.

Her husband put down his drink and walked up to the window. 'The man's an arse. An arrogant and headstrong arse who lacks the imagination to realise he's in the wrong. He's learnt nothing from what happened to his sons. Nothing, I tell you. I've saddled horses with more sense than him. He hears nothing apart from what he wants to hear and sees nothing except what he wants to see . . .'

Zayets ground his teeth and cast a glance at the darkening silhouette leaving the end of his drive. The figure waved an arm as a parting gesture and Zayets lifted his hand half-heartedly.

Natalia stroked his back and whispered, 'Don't worry, Grishka. They won't let him get away with it. How could they?'

Zayets, his tired eyes burning with frustration, pushed his wife's hand away. 'I'm not so sure. People like him, they always . . .'

Natalia looked at him tenderly.

'. . . get away with it. They always get away with it.'

Copic had enjoyed holding out on Zayets and making him squirm. It served him right for mentioning his sons; normally this would have resulted in a stand-up argument, but Copic sensed this was not the time for showing one's cards. Far better for him to let Zayets believe whatever he liked than entertain the risk of more lectures by disagreeing with him. In the end it was all just talk anyway – it would be decisions and not words which would decide his fate.

Copic tripped and stumbled over the remains of a snow stack. He was having trouble keeping his balance. The icy wind had started again and, to his irritation, he realised that he had left his gloves on Zayets' worktop.

'Fuck it,' he mumbled, and pressed his hands deep into his pockets. His decision not to go back to the chalet was tinged with guilt and anger at his bumbling carelessness; the gloves had been a present from his wife, his wife who was now dead. Copic felt a tear turn to ice and stick to the side of his face like wet glass. Here he was, left behind by the ones he loved with only football and booze for consolation, and now one of these was to be taken from him too.

A young soldier hurried past him, his face bent down against the oncoming wind. Predictably the boy in uniform reminded Copic of his sons, his two boys whom he had failed to protect. He wished he knew what had happened to them, whether they had joined their mother in death or whether they were still alive, being held in a camp somewhere awaiting trial. Both of them had been tearaways who, like true selfish bastards, had lived for themselves without a thought for their parents. When news had reached him that they had been arrested in Tiflis after being implicated in theft of equipment from an oil refinery, he had not been surprised. What had surprised him was when these charges were dropped and changed to high treason and espionage on behalf of a foreign power. Vasily, the younger of the two boys, was accused of spying on behalf of Germany and Italy while Sergei was jailed for being a British agent. Of course, everyone said the charges were ridiculous, but they had to be invented to save the boys from the shame of being convicted for their true crime – membership of the Left Opposition. In all honesty, Copic had found this as hard to swallow as the accusations of espionage. His boys may have been drunkards, braggarts and whore-masters, but they were not political rebels, let alone followers of the exile Trotsky. Still, the authorities, and his own upbringing, had told him that people did not get arrested for nothing, and dark talk spread that the boys had been involved in everything from white slavery to the sabotage of public works. In his heart Copic knew that it was this, and not the cholera, which had finally done for his wife earlier that year. He knew it, but found it too painful to face up to, so he had done what he had always done – drunk vodka and talked football, burying his agony under three trophies and two league cups. Meanwhile the fate of his sons remained whispered and uncertain, just like his own fate now, he reflected.

Pulling his hood up over his ears, he began the long walk down Potemkin Hill, the city humming below him like a large electrical plant working through the night.

Down on the Nevsky Prospect Kasper looked up at the scattering of lights on Potemkin Hill and wondered what the city must look like from up there. He often found himself looking at things in this way, but had only just started to understand why. First he would concentrate on the object and the accompanying thought. Then he would forget the thought and, through the force of his concentration, bleed into the object entirely, freeing himself from his own perspective and immersing himself in the lights, the clouds, or whatever it was that he was looking at. At this point he would feel his heart lift and he would rise, up through his body and into an air-like collection of sensations that the priests called spirit. However, as first-choice goalkeeper in a successful football team, he found it hard to spend too much time talking to his teammates about this.

'Hurry up, Kasper,' called Makhno from the other side of the tramlines. 'When you've stopped talking to God the rest of us would like to go and get pissed.'

'Of course, I'm sorry,' said Kasper. 'I was drifting again.'

Slovo rushed up behind him, leapt up on his back and tugged him down into the snow. Within seconds he was at the bottom of a five-man bundle, struggling for breath, cursing his friends and failing to see the funny side. Things were only brought to a close when the imposing figure of Big Koba threatened to make the five-man bundle six. Kasper was the only one not to get out of the way in time. Despite the consensus that Koba was no more than a jolly great giant, Kasper had long harboured thoughts to the contary, and as he rubbed his bruised leg he suddenly realised why; Koba was the only member of the team that he, or any of the other players, had yet to argue with. It would be a long while before Kasper grasped the full significance of this thought, by which time it would be too late for Koba, and no use to Kasper.

'Come on, Daddy-long-legs,' said Makhno, picking Kasper up off the floor. 'Old Koba here says he knows a place we can go on to.'

Kasper nodded sullenly, only too aware of the dangers of admitting, in present company, that he had wanted an early night.

Tomsky did not know what Muerta was doing, or what was going through her head as she did it, but it felt wonderful. For the past half-hour she had run her hair, nose, tongue or breasts, and maybe all of them, against his back in a light sweeping motion. He wanted to turn around and say thank you but was too relaxed, and besides, he was afraid that acknowledgement of what was happening would spoil it in some way.

'My throat's dry,' she said at last. 'I'm going to get some water. Do you want any?'

'Mmmm,' murmured Tomsky.

He felt Muerta lift her prominent front off his back, fiddle around for a towel, decide not to bother, and leave for the kitchen. Turning over on his side, he stared across the room at the high window slats and the snowflakes gathering on the scaffolding outside. He was happy, not just with Muerta but also, absurdly, with everything else, even his former unhappiness. This, and any other misfortune that had befallen him, suddenly seemed worth it, if only for allowing him to appreciate this moment and the bliss of the last few hours more fully. He was aware that there was something biblical about this thought, something that reeked of the old man in the sky, destiny and other things he did not believe in, but, for once, he did not care about being consistent. He had been waiting for something that was not already in his life to come in from the outside and change it. Muerta, as well as being a great girl with big tits, could be that change, just as coming back to Russia and accepting the job with Copic had been. Tomsky could feel a rising sense of freedom emanate from this realisation and, though it was strangely beautiful to feel this way, he knew it was also dangerous. It left him unprepared for the other decision he would have to make, one that could affect all this and everything else too.

In a few seconds Muerta would be next to him again. He could remember the night before and the cold he had felt in bed alone when she was not there; it was not a feeling that he wanted to experience again soon. Or her either, he hoped.

Klimt Grotsky was as pissed as only the chief of the secret police dared get. Crashing through the doors of his apartment block, he stumbled straight through the foyer and into the waiting lift cage.

'Take me up, you fuck,' he groaned at the bell-boy as

he threw himself into the corner and tried, despite his drunkenness, to remember who he had got drunk with.

'What are you looking at, boy?' he said as he forgot what it was he was trying to remember. 'Are you looking at this?' He leered as he tried to pull his squashed penis out of his trousers. 'I bet you want . . .'

Grotsky stopped. A terrible memory was beginning to arise out of the void. It began earlier in the day during a routine interrogation of an informant, a skinny little guy with a shaved head and freckles. Grotsky covered his face in an attempt to hide the shame, for it was nothing less than shame he was feeling. Not for beating the boy brutally, that was fair game, but for getting a woody as he did it, an obvious and fully formed erection through his leather strides. The kid had seen it and, in that slightly mad way doomed people have of sealing their fate, had started to laugh. By the time Cretor had entered the room 'mid-interrogation' Grotsky had the boy's head between his thighs, the lower half of his body kicking from side to side as it entered the last stages of suffocation. There was a saying that 'anything goes in the NKVD', but this last incident, even by the standards of the secret police, was pushing it, and Grotsky knew it. This would be (unless he could think of a way of killing Cretor, which he could, but unfortunately he still needed him for the football) yet another thing Cretor could hold against him, along with God knows what else his ex-wife had passed on through pillow talk.

The bell-boy carefully pulled open the metal gauze

and let Grotsky crawl out, omitting to mention to the police chief that he had just vomited over his leathers, and most of the lift as well.

Picking himself up, and wondering how he had climbed the steps so quickly, Grotsky kicked open his front door and marched into the bedroom. Under the impression that he had found the shower, Grotsky did what he would normally do in the toilet and, wondering where all the water had gone, collapsed into the 'bath'.

He woke up five minutes later with a raging thirst, his mouth tasting, for reasons he could not fully fathom, of onions. Then suddenly it struck him – he had told Lotya to leave her apartment and be here tonight, just in case he came home and felt frisky, which he was.

Lotya, where the fucking hell are you? he thought, angry that she could not hear him, especially when he was thinking so loudly.

Pulling down the Venetian partition he had procured from the house of a dead Italian communist, arrested on his orders, Grotsky pawed his way through the living room into the area that had served as a games room for the apartment's former inhabitants. There he found Lotya sitting happily on the floor doing a jigsaw puzzle.

'Make me come,' he spluttered.

Uncomplainingly Lotya did what was asked of her, Grotsky reciting his usual plethora of curses and oaths as he held her by the ears. Finally, and much to his and her relief, he came. He was just sorry that it was over

Lotya's chin and not in the arse of a big fat cow like his second wife.

Lotya wiped the jism off her face and gently stepped over Grotsky, who had collapsed on the floor in tears, as was often his wont after 'sex'. She knew better than to try to comfort him, and anyway, it didn't really interest her – she had a puzzle to finish and a pile of other ones she had found in the cupboard to do later.

When Lotya came back into the room, an hour later, to help him to bed, he was fast asleep. Carefully, and with practice, she rubbed the cloth soaked in her urine through his eyebrows, over his head, and along his mouth. Then, with great difficulty, she pulled him into the bedroom, covered him in his coat and let him sleep on the floor, careful to take her place next to him when, in a few hours, he would wake and remember nothing.

# Chapter Seven

## Wednesday

Radek did not know whether he had slept lightly or heavily. His head was full of half-remembered conversations, too practical to have been dreams, and yet he had no recollection of leaving his room, or even his bed, for the past ten hours. Of course, since all these conversations had occurred with Katya, in various happier locations, they would have to have been dreams, and this thought was enough to snuff out what life the simple act of waking up had imbued in him.

More in hope than in wonder, Radek stared out at the slowly assembling colours of the early morning sky, and tried to think less self-centred thoughts. These mainly involved Tomsky, Copic and the football team and, to a lesser and more sentimental extent, his parents. It was not hard for each of these roads to lead back to Katya, but, for a moment, Radek tried to stop them from doing so. Of course, he knew that his presence was vital to the team if victory were to be guaranteed against Dynamo on Saturday. Radek, no matter how damaged he may have been in other respects, was nothing if not confident of his footballing abilities, and although he realised it had been nice of Tomsky not to bring the subject up, it was obvious to Radek that this thought must weigh heavily on the minds of his teammates. If he thought of his situation from the point of view of someone else, it was possible to envisage a swift return to first-team football, but the trouble was that it was not easy for him to think like this over a sustained period of time. Within seconds Katya would reappear within the folds of each thought, laughing at him for daring to take anything else seriously. Deep inside him, he knew that he was not only being unfair to his friends but also that it was deeply unmanly of him to behave in this way. Katya and life had not failed him, rather, he had failed them, and this could, without much further reflection, be summed up by the fact that he not left his bed for the past ten hours.

Radek coughed into his hand and glanced in the mirror; the last thing he needed to add to his list of woes was self-loathing. It was bad enough remembering every last detail of his time with Katya and poring over each moment for some answer that could explain why she was not here now. The two memories of the moment (they changed from hour to hour) focused on the questions of why she had cried after returning home on her first day at work and why she shouted at him every time he tried to sing to her. If only he could solve these mysteries, he could then write to her and perhaps things would improve . . .

Tomsky shook the chair gently. Copic half opened an eye, surveyed what he could bear of the scene, and pulled the coat over his head.

'Oh, Jesus Christ,' he groaned. Two empty bottles of vodka and a case of cheap aftershave lay underneath his desk.

'It looks as though you had quite a party,' said Tomsky. 'Did any of the other guests make it?'

'Satan's blood, you sadistic cunt, fetch me some water before I die,' whined the helpless Copic.

'There's some here,' said Tomsky, thrusting a jug into Copic's outstretched hand. 'You must have been using it as a mixer . . . So what brought you back here last night?'

'I didn't want to go back to that flat,' said Copic, emptying the jug over his head. 'No law against that, I hope?'

'Not that I know of, but still, this isn't the most salubrious place you could have chosen to sleep over.'

Copic grunted and wrapped the soaking coat around his head like a towel. It was obvious that the gap between the two men's moods was cataclysmic. While Tomsky could smell Muerta's warmth all over his face, Copic was struggling to have any sense of smell at all. Nevertheless, the professional hangover survivalist in him would not allow this temporary indisposition to last any longer than it had to.

'I'll go down in a minute, have a shower and get my tracksuit on, then get something to eat before practice starts. What time is it, anyway?'

'Don't worry, it's only nine. Here, have some more water.'

Copic took the refilled jug with both hands and

this time attempted to drink some. Despite a violent coughing fit he succeeded in getting most of it down his throat.

'How did it go with Zayets last night?' Tomsky asked cautiously, aware that this may have been the reason behind Copic's choice of nightcap. 'I don't know about you, but despite finding out that the situation isn't as clear cut as we were first told, I'm still very worried. I think I played things down too much yesterday . . .'

'Zayets . . .' Copic put his hand up to his forehead. 'You know how it is, how they end up . . . those bastards who choose the path of least intensity, all smugly tucked up in bed by nine o'clock with their little wifeys . . .'

In truth Copic could hardly remember a word of what had been said all evening – he just knew that things weren't, in one way, as bad as he thought they might be, but in another way were much worse. The bad bit was to do with everything in his life being predicated on necessary falsehoods, the good bit about his life not being in any immediate danger, though for all he knew it might have been the other way around. If he could only remember the moment before he had fallen asleep, that point at which everything had come together and he had unearthed the answer . . . But it was no good; it was all too far away from him now.

'So he just went over what he'd said in the morning, did he?'

'Pretty much . . . I mean, it was more or less the same thing but not exactly the same, if you see what

I mean. To be honest I found the whole thing quite confusing. The man speaks in riddles just like everyone is learning to these days. I'm not saying it's wrong, if that's your job, but Zayets . . . he used to be my friend.'

'In what way did you not understand what he was talking about?' persisted Tomsky. 'It's important that you get this right . . .'

'No, I did understand him, I'm just not absolutely sure that I did. No, let me put it to you in another way. I knew but not with any certainty . . . knowledge without certainty, anything else is irresponsible speculation. That's what I said to him last night,' said Copic, back on track again.

'But what did he say to you?'

'For God's sake, man! Stop asking me all these bloody questions. Can't you see that my head's banging and I'm ready to dance with Mr Death!'

Tomsky smiled understandingly and offered his boss a cigarette.

'Of course not, not in my state, not for a moment or two anyway.'

'Can I ask you one more thing . . .'

'What?'

'I thought Zayets might have told you that the whole thing was a giant misunderstanding, since as a rule people prefer to lay the blame for arguments on misunderstandings, rather than their friends. That is if the arguments are not big enough to fall out over.'

'No. He definitely didn't do that.'

'The reason I say this is because Zayets said far more to us than my informant would verify. My guy said yes, it's true, people *are* pissed off with us, but we're not in so much trouble that we'd have to throw the game on Saturday. At least, not yet.'

A sudden twitch of recognition flickered across Copic's face. 'I remember a bit of that, yes, I think I can remember a bit of that. We might get into a bit of trouble or we might not, but Zayets *definitely* will, that's what he said. He said that it's his arse on the line first, and then ours.'

'Then that's more or less what I heard, but it still doesn't make it true. I can't believe Grotsky would risk making himself look ridiculous over something like this, but if Zayets wants to believe his threats then it's his call. He's panicking because he's getting in bed with the comrades now and doesn't want us embarrassing him every weekend. Do you think that might be it?'

'Well then, what have *we* got to worry about? We're no better or worse off than before.'

'No, we *are* worse off, just better off than we thought we were when . . .' Tomsky rolled his eyes; he was doing a Copic. 'What I mean is that we don't normally think we'll get in trouble just for playing football whereas now there's a chance we might. Which, though a lot worse than normal, is still better than what Zayets . . .'

'All right, all right! I get the picture! Christ, you

like to bang on, don't you? Is it only with me or does everyone get the same treatment? And anyway, what was it I said to you in the first place? Knowledge without certainty, wasn't it? Well then, what's wrong with that for a policy?'

'And that's what you want me to tell the players today, when it comes to explaining this whole thing to them?'

Copic paused. 'The players . . . hmm . . . that's a whole different matter that needs to be considered separately from the rest of this. Yes, things change a bit when you bring them into the equation. You see, what I'm trying to say is that I'm not sure whether they really need to know about this. I mean, what good would it do? It would only worry them and put them off their game.'

'You're wrong. It's got as much to do with them as us.'

'But . . .'

'It has. Think about it. Of course it has.'

'I know you're right in a way, but it's just that there're so many of them to tell, and if we tell them, do we then have to tell the back room staff, the ball boys and the groundsman? And what are we meant to actually say to them? It's not as though we *really* know what's going on ourselves, or even know what we're going to do next . . .'

'Knowledge without certainty, that's our slogan . . .'

'Don't give me that crap . . .'

'But if we were going to throw the game, if that's

what we decide to do, then we'd have to tell them then, wouldn't we? How could we not?'

'Well, I don't know whether we are going to throw the game now . . .'

'I certainly don't want to.'

'Then tell a few of the senior players, ask them what they think, do it tonight at that party they're holding at Radek's.'

'That's a good idea, then tomorrow we'll make the final decision.'

Tomsky winced as he said this. Last night he had told Muerta everything. It was his guess that the senior players, and almost everyone else, would have made their minds up about the matter long before he raised the issue at Radek's party that night.

'Good, we're rolling again,' said Copic, shaking the coat-towel free of his head. 'Now all I need to do is stodge up and then we'll be ready to go out and kick some arse.'

The door opened behind them and Tomsky felt the seasonal draught, carried through corridors when two people fall in love in autumn, fill the room.

'Haven't you heard of knocking, you great white witch?'

'I'm sorry,' said Muerta Astro, incapable of stopping herself from laughing, 'but I thought Comrade Tomsky would want these.' She raised his tracksuit bottoms over her head, last used as a prop at her flat the night before, and waved them like a flag.

'Satan's saucy boils, I've had to put up with some

cheeky stuff in my time but this really takes the weevil. Tomsky, get out, you're a fucking disgrace, man, a fucking disgrace.'

Suppressing his laughter like an infant, Tomsky crossed the room and made a face at Muerta, who made one back. With his head bent down, and holding in his giggles, he whispered, 'I can't believe you did that.'

Muerta flashed a toothy smile and shrugged her shoulders, her face answerless and happy.

'You two look like you've just made the decision to lose your jobs and enjoy life, but believe me, the tests are still to come, then you'll see . . .' Copic called after them, unsure whether to express outrage or ignore Tomsky's barefaced triumphalism, his irritation quickly giving way to hunger and the thought of a breakfast of oatcakes, brandy and brandy butter. 'You'll see,' he muttered, thinking of how he would like his eggs prepared. 'Go without the essentials for a few days and you'll see.'

He licked his chops greedily and got up to go to the team canteen, thoughts of this forthcoming feast blinding him to the speed with which two people could banish a problem without really solving it.

Her bare feet landed on the hard rubber floor with a sensual thump. Behind her a train of girls, aged twelve to twenty-one, took their turns to vault over the great suede gym horse. Lotya, by far the oldest, though looking no more than fourteen in the harsh white light, bent down to adjust the plaster around her narrow ankle. Out of the corner of her eye she could see the figure of Slovo in the visitors' gallery, standing out like an alien amongst the elastic, talcum powder and perspiration of female under-twenty-one gymnastics. Not giving a damn whether anyone saw her, she waved at him frantically and pointed to the clock, her wrist and the exit. The other girls continued to throw powder over their hands and swing on bars as if nothing had happened.

Slovo, for his part, was overcome with shock. He had already, without even realising it, given up on any hope of Lotya ever knowing who he was, let alone actually acknowledging him. Instead he had stoically prepared himself to return to the same spot on the balcony every day, and silently admire her from this vantage point of unobserved safety. Gratification was too much for him to even consider, whereas steady and controllable disappointment fell well within his methods of coping with the world. But Lotya motioning to him like an excited usherette threw all this into turmoil. It was, as it would turn out, the start of a new life.

His first words were 'I know who you are' and hers were 'So will you help me kill him?' Slovo was not allowed any more time to feel nervous. Lotya talked so quickly, and he listened so attentively, that by the time she had finished he was ready to do whatever she asked of him. This was, if anything, as great a surprise to her as it was to him. Grotsky had frequently criticised Lotya for being passive and uncommunicative during those few society occasions they had attended together, and it was true that her natural chattiness had deserted her since her move to Moscow. She simply found it hard to talk to people who obviously considered her to be their next girlfriend at best, or insignificant, and on her way out tomorrow, at worst. But with Slovo it was different. Here was someone she felt she could tell everything to, and not just things she knew but things she wanted to happen and had not even dreamed of yet. The fact that he hung on her every word like a faithful retriever confirmed her deepest intuition, which was that in some oblique way he already knew her, and by the end of her monologue she had confided in him completely, until she felt utterly drained. The relief was so great that she went farther than she would even have dared contemplate, and asked, in not so many words, for him to rescue her. Despite the abstract nature of what she was asking him to do, at least as far as concrete plans were concerned, she had never felt more practical, or empowered over anything, in her life before.

Pressing her tiny hand into his, she asked, 'Then tomorrow, will you meet me again?'

He nodded mutely and she was gone. It had all happened, and was finished, far faster than he could comprehend. He had tried to tell her that he was not the world's most practical man when it came to executing hastily assembled plans, but she did not seem to mind. Instead she had replied that practical men were of no use to her, all they could do was make short-term calculations based on immediate gain and thus achieve nothing of lasting substance. What she wanted was a brave man, and she could tell he was one of those. He did not have much trouble agreeing with her, and so it was decided; he would become her accomplice and lover-in-waiting. It was mad to think that all he had hoped for was a glimpse of her from the visitors' balcony, one that she would not even have been aware of. And yet it had seemed as if she had already *known* who he was, which meant something in itself. Perhaps this was the way with life, Slovo reflected, that once it had started moving it would charge ahead quickly, where only months earlier, with plenty of time on his hands, it had refused to go anywhere at all. His conclusion was simple; some moments in life were important and others were not.

Walking briskly away from the side entrance of the gym, his head held high in the air but his legs still shaking with happy bewilderment, Slovo wondered what his hair would look like once he had let it grow again. That he would was no longer in question, though whether it would grow back like moss or be sharp and twig-like only time would reveal. What was important was that Lotya was sorry he had cut it and must therefore have recognised him without it. And this would not have been possible if she had not spent a considerable amount of time thinking about him first. So this, decided Slovo, was what something being too good to be true felt like. Oblivious to the other pedestrians, he strolled on to the main path and punched the head off a snowman, mildly frustrated that there were no pebbles he could kick; he was feeling vital, playful and young, put out only by the fact that his would have to remain a necessarily secret passion.

Makhno raised him off the ground like a lanky Cossack tackling a lost farm animal. 'You've chosen a funny route to training this morning, haven't you, little man? Don't you lodge with Kasper on the other side of the river?'

'Perhaps he's decided to become a gymnast,' said the handsome woman beside him, 'or maybe he's just working on his lower body strength,' she added, pointing to the gym.

Slovo cringed. Makhno and his sister, Vera, a laundry woman for the team, had an uncanny way of pre-empting other people's affairs, just at that point at which they were about to become fully fledged secrets.

'I was just drifting, Comrades. My head hurt after last night's drinking and I needed a walk.'

Makhno grinned and picked up a clump of snow. 'When my head hurts I eat a handful of this stuff.'

'Don't listen to him,' said his Vera, 'he enjoys handing on useless advice. He thinks it brings him closer to the Party.'

Slovo flinched a little. Although he had just agreed to kill one of the Party's most senior figures, the Makhno family's semi-open disrespect for Party protocol still made him nervous out of habit.

'There's Babel' – Makhno pointed – 'going the same

way as us just like he does every bloody day. Why doesn't he ever slow down and let us walk with him?'

'He probably leaves his apartment five minutes early every morning to avoid that possibility,' replied Vera.

'Perhaps he's just shy,' offered Slovo. 'I used to be a bit like that. Finding it difficult to talk to people you don't already know.'

'Well, no one would get to know anyone if we all thought like that. Let's find out. Hey! Babel, old boy! Wait for us!' shouted Makhno.

Babel, who had been pretending they were not there, turned the corner and practically ran over the tramlines, losing himself among the crowds of traders and pedlars on their way to Pawski Market.

Tailing him was the secret policeman, who now turned his attention to the happy triumvirate responsible for causing him to lose his charge. Makhno, recognising the man at once, called on him to join them too, thus forcing him to take the same path as Babel across the tramlines.

'Funny man, that. No sense of the fitness of things. The same problem as Comrade Babel, really – you spend too long in the Party and you forget how to mix with the rest of us proles down on the farm.'

Slovo nodded politely, his eyes fixed on a plane flying through the rising morning mist, its wings shaking nervously. It looked as if it had been made out of tin and glue, its very ability to fly a miracle that ought to be cautiously celebrated. 'I'd like to be on that,' he said without thinking, omitting to add that he would like to be on it with Lotya, a bag full of money and a ticket to another life.

'Why? You don't even know where it's going. It might land in Siberia for all you know.'

'I just want to be on it, that's all.'

The plane disappeared behind a stack of clouds, and the three walked on for the rest of the way listening to Makhno talk about the pointlessness of air travel.

Grotsky caught all four of the jailers by complete surprise when he practically fell through the door of their office.

'Which one of my cells is free?' he bawled.

'Prisoner Rubashov is ready and waiting for interrogation in Cell 101, sir!' answered the chief jailer, standing to attention.

'I don't give a virgin's palsy for Rubashov or any damned interrogation. I asked which of the cells is free, which *doesn't have anyone in it*, you understand me?'

Looking slightly startled, the chief jailer made eyes at his clerk, who quickly ran over to the key board.

'Sorry to say there are no free cells on this floor, sir. We've got 'em packed in eight to a cell like sardines.'

'Well, clear one of them.'

'Begging your pardon, sir, but what are we to do with the prisoners? The whole Lubyanka's heaving . . .'

'Take them out into the courtyard and shoot them or throw them into the Volga and drown them. I don't care so long as the nearest cell to this office is empty by the time I've got back from having a shit. Understood?'

'Sir!'

Grotsky hobbled through the office and into the adjoining toilet. His whole body was aching like a giant bruise. Dropping his trousers, he sat down to make himself comfortable, oblivious to the patches of liquid squashed between his thighs and the seat. The toilet was a place where he deliberately liked to keep his head blank so as to concentrate more fully on the job in hand, and in this wish he was not disappointed. By the time he had walked back into the office, fifteen minutes later, he could truly say that nothing had crossed his mind in the intervening time.

'The cell's empty?'

'Yes, sir! Here are the keys, sir.'

Grotsky snatched the keys and pushed his way past the jailers into the lamplit corridor. He hated, and yet felt reassured by, the absence of natural light along these dark corridors of the Lubyanka Prison. They reminded him of the seminary in Tiflis, the one he had hated as a boy but grown to love in memory. He had been sent there by the family of a well-to-do local merchant who had taken him out of the orphanage and saved him from a life of destitution. It was there that he had first read Victor Hugo, Voltaire and Plekhanov. By the end of his first year he was an agnostic and by the end of the second a committed atheist. Together, and behind closed doors, he and the merchant's daughter had discovered the revolutionary pamphlets of the underground printing press, and by his seventeenth birthday they had taught each other the ABC of communism. In the long summer of 1912 both of them had slept in the great wheat fields of Odessa, overlooking the Caspian Sea, and sworn everlasting love over a battered copy of *Moby-Dick*, and with it their faith in the creation of a new world free of violence, poverty and oppression.

Grotsky pushed open the cell door and flung himself down on to the narrow lice-infested cot. Touching his temples, he drew his legs up and regressed into a fetal position.

The seminary was no different to this place, he reflected, perhaps a little better, though probably not much. At least the Lubyanka was not run by monks, sadistic perverts no better than Turks, drunk in this life and dead for ever in the next. Grotsky allowed himself the ghost of a smile. He had arrested and shot his fair share of monks, holy men and other servants of God. Not one had succeeded in making him feel small or guilty about his duty. He shuddered slightly. Guilt was not a concept he cared to entertain lest he find too much of it in an unexpected place. He stared up at the black brick ceiling of the cell and saw the bent and twisted body of Mitya, his first and only love, being dragged away in a tattered sack. He rubbed his eyes and looked again. It seemed as though the whole ceiling was moving towards him. One by one faces were emerging through the bricks, the cracks between them forming the blood line of a single accusatory body striding downwards, its bony finger pointing at Grotsky like the scythe carried by the angel of death.

He could see Mitya's father, the merchant who had loved him like his own son, then Dzerzhinsky, his old political master whose legacy he had now betrayed. Next was Copic's son Vasily, who had refused to incriminate his own father and whom Grotsky had dispatched with his own hand. Each yelled their story at him and asked the same question; why did you murder us? But Grotsky was deaf to their voices. All he could hear were the cries of his first love Mitya, killed by his desire to protect her,

'Mitya, forgive me, forgive me. Ignorant evil bastard that I am!'

It had been the winter of 1921. Seven years had passed since his adopted father had disowned him, the seminary expelled him, and the army drafted his unwilling body to fight the Austrians in Galicia. In that time he had come to know the true meaning of pain, first lying with his own fear in a slit trench for three years, too scared to touch the flapping hearts of his dismembered friends, their bodies scattered amidst the black smoke that would rise from the charred earth after every artillery bombardment. Then came the horrors of the Civil War, a time in which the embodiment of every base human evil was granted a political position and, in some cases, a uniform and a title. Grotsky was awarded the Order of the Red Banner and a silver wristwatch for his part in the defence of Leningrad. Trotsky himself mentioned him in dispatches and gave him his own cavalry detachment to chase Baron Wrangel back to the Crimea and into the Black Sea. This he achieved with consummate ease, the scar across his forearm evidence of his heroism in battle and willingness to lead from the front. Finally the day came, just as Grotsky knew it would, when the Red Guards stopped their horses at the gates of Tiflis and were told that, as a reward for their routing of the White Army, every man would be given complete impunity to do as he wished in those districts of the city deemed bourgeois. Grotsky had ridden straight to the house of his true love and shot her as she opened the door to him. From what he witnessed over the next forty-eight hours, she had been one of the lucky ones.

The door slowly edged open and Cretor tiptoed in. 'I thought I'd find you in here,' he said.

Grotsky made no reply.

'You're a deep one, Chief, coming in here to meditate like this . . .'

'You only had to ask one of the guards where I was, you toad.'

'The guards? I didn't think of them. No, my policeman's intuition told me you were here . . . you like to think about things, don't you? Maybe I'm wrong, I don't know, perhaps you're just conscientious about checking on cell conditions for our prisoners . . .'

Grotsky did not bother to reply.

Cretor bit his lip. The cell smelt of weasel's piss and old newspapers, its floor at least five inches deep in water.

'How did it go with the Boss?'

'The Boss? Gorfsky could have told you by now. Why do you have to come in here and trouble me?'

'Because Gorfsky said you stayed on alone with him at the end of the briefing to talk about something.'

'Yeah, we talked all right. We talked about organising football teams for the artillery, the aviation school and the navy. His fucking son wants to get in on the act and have a team of his own.'

'You're joking.'

'No. What's there to joke about? The Boss thinks we've been doing so badly that we've left the way open for that little prick Vasily.'

'Jesus Christ, who'd have thought it? And what else did he say?'

'He thinks Bukharin is a swine or even worse than a swine . . .'

'Tell me something I don't already know . . .'

'He wants to send dear old Sergo to Japan as a warning in case he gets carried away in Georgia, and he's worried about agitation at union meetings . . .'

'Brilliant. So did you tie that in with the Spartak situation?'

'I tried to but he wouldn't let me. You know him, he's a cunning bastard who likes to take the long way round . . .'

Grotsky hesitated and then decided against going on – it was probably a mistake to have called Stalin a cunning bastard in front of Cretor, just as much as it was to let him believe he needed him as a shoulder to unburden himself upon.

'Personally I think you might have missed a chance there. If you could have just got him to agree to arresting a handful of their players before the game . . .'

'You don't *set* an agenda when you're with the Boss; you just follow one. His one.'

'But you know how to handle him . . .'

Grotsky snorted, his guard down again. 'Perhaps once, when he needed my help, back in the days when we still had to have a reason to arrest someone. Maybe then I did know how to handle him. But not now, no one can now.'

Cretor laughed. 'A reason to arrest someone? I never knew you were such a humanist!'

'You idiot,' sneered Grotsky, 'what do you know? You who were born to pick pockets and sell whores, you dare to tell me about humanism or any other kind of ism? What the fuck do you know?'

'I'm sorry, sir, I thought I was being funny.'

'You may think you could do my job better than me, but I tell you, the Boss would crush you like a worm. You haven't got what it takes to last a single second in his company. Our leader isn't a man who appreciates initiatives from below.'

'I only . . .'

'No. Shut up and listen. Think of the world you're in now, just as my assistant, and then multiply it by ten thousand times. Then add to it the fact that, in this new world, you'll never know where you stand in relation to anyone or anything else and break this down into an equation where you're privy to the whims of the world's most powerful man. Done it? Well, if you have you're not even close to the job I have to do every day. Last week the boss wanted to talk to me about football. So we talked about football. In fact, now I come to think of it, football was the only thing we talked about. If you were to walk into the room and listen to us you'd think you were hearing Russia's greatest football fanatics holding forth. But then, when I raised the subject this week, after he'd finished talking about Vasily, and tried to tell him what I've been planning as regards Copic and his gang, he lifted his hand up and told me to shut up. Then he says, completely contradicting what's gone before, that when I'm playing football he's trying to run a country, that politics is what counts and not some ball game for delinquents . . .'

Cretor flinched. 'That's not good.'

'You're damned right.'

'So what are you going to do now?'

Grotsky said nothing and turned over on his side.

Cretor stared into his jagged reflection, broken between the puddles on the floor, and tried to ignore the screams from the interrogation room which echoed down the corridor.

'What are we going to do now?'

'Leave me alone.'

The screams stopped and Cretor heard a voice protesting its innocence. He recognised it at once: Dmitri Polker, ringmaster of the Moscow State Circus.

'I wonder what we brought him in for,' he thought out aloud.

'For not taking a hint.'

Cretor walked out and closed the door behind him.

'Comrade Tomsky, Comrade Irena Polya will see you now.'

So that was her second name, Irena, he had forgotten it. To the team she had simply been known as Radek's Katya. Tomsky smiled. No wonder she had wanted to get out and start a new life.

'Tomsky.'

'Hello, Katya.'

Her office was like a large surgery; so different from the cramped warehouse space she had worked in as a junior functionary. The well-cut green uniform she was wrapped in seemed to suit the new station she had attained without, Tomsky felt, dimming any of her girlish appeal.

'What is it you do now?' he asked.

'Funny, isn't it, you can remember the position of even the most insignificant player but when it comes to remembering the jobs of people who do real work you lot are always at a loss. Do you do it on purpose or did nature just make you that way?'

Tomsky smiled falteringly. It was obvious Katya was in no mood to be nice to a man she associated with a life she was well rid of.

'Well, whatever it is you do it must be something quite important,' he continued, ignoring her warlike glow. 'But of course, I probably wouldn't understand all the ins and outs of it. I'm useless at desk work.'

'If you've come here to insult me then you're already doing a brilliant job.'

'Please, that's crazy, what are you being so defensive for?'

'Because I know what you and that fat idiot Copic are all about. You only ever turn up when you want something from someone. Well, I'm not like Radek, you can't use me like you use him.'

'Jesus Christ, woman, what did the Devil put in your soup this morning? I've only come here to talk . . .'

'I don't see what we could possibly have to talk about.'

'*Possibly have to talk about* . . . are these the airs and graces they teach you in the NKVD, Katya?'

'I'm not in the NKVD, I'm part of a government organisation . . .'

'I don't care what you're in, all you "comrades" are the same. It doesn't make any difference if you're arranging files or pulling the trigger, you all bow before the same logic.'

'I think you'd better leave.'

'I'm going. To hell with you.'

Once outside her office Tomsky felt like a fucking fool. He had not had an exchange like that since he had left the woman he thought he would marry in America, three years earlier. And with her he had at least had six months to build up to it. He felt his pulse; it was racing out of control. He had probably raised his voice, maybe even shouted. In two minutes he had managed to hurt someone he barely knew, damage his own dignity and no doubt increase his short-term chances of being sent to prison. There was no point in being proud about this – he would have to go back in, say he was sorry and take whatever else she had to hand out.

He edged open the door and, without looking at her, said through the gap, 'I apologise. I'm supposed to be an expert at man management but all I've done is upset you and act like an idiot . . .'

'Oh, shut up and sit down.'

To his relief Katya was not vengeful, just very upset. It was, he would shamefully reflect later, the first time he had been able to obtain a foothold in her, see past her glacial beauty and talk to her properly; something circumstances would never permit again.

She had lit a cigarette and was shaking her head, half crying and half laughing in a way more reminiscent of a nervous young girl than a leading Party administrator.

'So you came here because of Radek. I suppose he sent you here. I can't see you coming of your own accord. Not with that nice office of yours to lounge around in all day.'

Resisting the urge to say something about bitterness, Tomsky gestured. 'But you've got a nice office too, much nicer than mine in fact . . .'

'Whatever. Get to the point. You want me to go back to him, don't you? That way he'll go on playing for your ridiculous football team instead of mulling around his flat like an old woman.'

'Why do you hate him so much?'

'Don't pretend to be interested in me or in what I think. Not one of you even bothered to contact me and ask me how I was when we broke up. No, it was all Radek . . .'

'It seemed like you could look after yourself.'

'As if you gave the matter any thought!'

'I did, but . . . I didn't think you, well, liked me, or any of the others, very much.'

'I didn't not like you,' said Katya, chewing the end of her cigarette.

Tomsky raised a hopeful eyebrow and smiled. Katya waved her hand, as if to dismiss the possibility of the conversation adopting a more cordial tone. 'All you need to know is that I'll never go back to him, and you can tell him that, that I'll never get back together again with him.'

'He won't like it but I've told him to expect nothing so I can't say he'll be surprised . . . he will be very hurt, though.'

'Oh, he hasn't got you feeling sorry for him, has he? He's very good at that, manipulating events so *you* end up looking like the one who's in the wrong.' She touched Tomsky's wrist and pinched it. 'It's like this. You think you're with this great big loveable bear who'll protect and look after you but then, when you're not looking, he'll turn around and bite you. Believe me, I loved him with all my heart but he was no prize catch – in fact, he was a backward selfish idiot, a weight I had to carry. You understand these things, working with that barrel Copic.'

Tomsky nodded and felt the beginnings of a smile. He wasn't sure whether it was because Katya, who had now established her superiority over him and the absent Radek, was softening a little, or because she was just pleased to have another chance to attack her former lover, but either way the atmosphere was lightening. For all her venom she had an appealing and forthright knack of showing interest without flirtation, and recognition without a single compliment.

'One thing he probably won't have told you was that it was his idea for us to part. I won't tell you why, I'll leave the washing of dirty laundry to him . . .'

'Katya, it's not hard to understand why you have your rehearsed set of grievances. Radek, in his own peculiar way, has them as well, but it's yourself you're punishing. I'm sure he'll always feel a tremendous guilt for his handling of you but . . .'

'Handling! I'm not a horse, Tomsky!'

'I'm sorry, I mean treatment . . . but I know he wants nothing more now than to make up and try again. Perhaps the best thing would be for the two of you to meet and talk to each other. After all, you haven't stopped talking about him so he must still mean something to you . . .'

'Yes, a complete waste of my time! Four years that I could have spent doing something else!' Katya's pony-tail shook like the spear of an ancient warrior queen, allowing Tomsky to understand why Radek put up with this; there was something thrilling about being attacked by such a beautiful woman. 'I don't ever want to see him again. He's in the past; we have nothing in common any more and nothing to say to each other. When I know what I want I'm fine, when I don't I'm in pieces. When I was with him I never knew what was going to happen next, and never really knew what I wanted. Now I do and I'm happy. So leave me alone and stop dragging up the past.' Her nose was twitching like a rabbit's. Tomsky remembered Radek mentioning this mannerism; how wonderful it looked when she was in love, and how frightening it looked when she wasn't. 'I don't live for Radek any more. I have my own life now and I don't want to go back to a past I don't care about.'

'You've a funny view of the past, Katya.'

'What do you mean?'

'If the past has no value for you then nor has the present.'

'Stop twisting! I know you're good at this, but *I* know what I think and you aren't going to make me believe otherwise.'

'You can believe what you want, but one thing I've noticed is that people who don't care about the past can never really commit themselves to the present moment, because before long it'll be just another part of the past they don't care about.'

Katya glared at him silently and put out her cigarette. 'Whatever, whatever you want to believe, Tomsky.'

'I must have got you wrong, Katya, because the person Radek described to me cared about things. Not loving him any more is one thing but going as far as . . .'

'Please would you just shut up and stop talking. Talk, talk, talk – all I can hear is you people talking.'

Tomsky waited for a moment then, seeing that Katya had nothing else to add, picked up his cap and walked to the door.

'One minute.'

'What?'

'You and Copic, all of you, you bring too much attention to yourselves.'

'What's that supposed to mean?'

'Nothing. Only that it would be better if you didn't.'

'Katya.'

'What?'

'One of the things I hate about being alive now, which might be one of the reasons why I won't be for much longer, is that since we all live in constant fear of arrest, little remarks like yours take on a cryptic meaning when left to rot in the imagination. That's why people who work for the security services are such smug bastards since all it takes for them to play God is a little quip like "It's not for you to ask questions like that" and the rest of us poor citizens are shitting chunks.'

'I'm not playing games with you, Tomsky. I'm trying to give you a warning.'

'Well, you'll have to try a bit harder because I don't know what you're talking about.'

'You're a bastard, aren't you?'

'I'm sorry, but if I am it's only because I'm addressing that part of you that makes me feel like being one.'

Katya laughed scornfully. 'So the rest of me is all right, then? I want you to know that the reason I'm telling you this is because of Radek. You're all he has now and if anything happened to you I won't be there to look after him.'

'Go on, then.'

'Blumkin, your kit man.'

'Cheerful guy, I know him.'

'He's an informer. They brought him in a fortnight ago and now he's working for them.'

'Blumkin? Is there anyone else?'

'Timoshenko, the masseur, perhaps Koba – no one else I know of.'

'Koba? Big Koba, you mean?' Tomsky drew a sharp breath as he felt an awful sense of recognition dawn on him; in one stroke Koba's all-pervasive smile had taken on a very different meaning.

'Yes. I hear he feeds them bullshit stories every week but sooner or later they'll apply the screws for something more tangible.'

'It's so hard to credit . . . but thank you. I suspected Timoshenko but I'm surprised, really surprised, about Koba. He's a simpleton from the provinces, but a good lad. There isn't a malevolent bone in his body . . . it's hard to understand how they could have got him into a position where he'd have to inform on his friends . . .'

'For someone who's been around the block you're

still terribly naive. You and Copic; your conversations were always too candid and public. You were both so open that some people even thought you were police agents trying to implicate them in criminal conversations. I could have told you that at the time and I barely knew either of you. Any one of the chats I overheard could have got you life on the Grand Canal.'

'I sort of suspected they might. Thank you for never reporting them.'

Katya snorted, 'As if I would have.' She tugged the band out of her hair, allowing her light brown locks to fall gently over her shoulders. 'There's another thing too, though even you must know about this already. The match on Saturday . . .'

'You're right, I do know. So much so that I'm pleased when I actually forget about the bloody thing.'

Katya smiled slightly. 'Well, what are you going to do? Doesn't Radek's indisposition come at a useful time? I mean, with him in bed it'll look more realistic if you lose.'

'If we did lose it would, yes.'

'But . . . but you might not?'

Tomsky said nothing.

'You really had better get out now. It would look suspicious if you stayed any longer.'

Tomsky nodded and, expecting no warm farewells, turned the handle on the door and was halfway out when he heard Katya say, 'Take care of yourself.'

\* \* \*

'Is that the players' lounge?'

'No, it's an NKVD torture chamber.'

'Makhno, just the man I wanted.'

'Where are you calling from?'

'From a booth in the main hall of the Ministry of Information.'

'How much did they offer you?'

'Listen to me, I'm serious; I need you to put the word out on Blumkin. I've just found out that he's been working for the comrades.'

'I won't need to. He cleared up and packed his bags on Monday and asked for a new assignment. Probably to go and spy on someone he hasn't made friends with yet.'

Tomsky whistled quietly. 'Strange, isn't it, when they do the honest thing like that.'

'Anything else I should know while we're on this happy subject?'

'There is something else but I think I'd better handle it myself.'

'Okay.'

'One other thing. Will you be seeing Radek later on?'

'I could do.'

'I'd appreciate it if you did. I've already had one session with him and it wouldn't do him any harm to hear this from you, if only because he'll be reluctant to make a scene if you're the one to tell him. I've talked to Katya, that's what I've been doing here, and I think it's safe to say that there's no way back for him, at least as far as she's concerned.'

'Got you.'

'Later.'

Tomsky put the receiver down and made his way out of the building as calmly as he could, careful not to look too pleased about having made a seditious phone call from a spot packed full of police informants. The entire hall resonated to the harsh undercurrent of whispers that bode no living thing any good, and it was a relief for Tomsky to walk out in one piece. Though not as much of one as he would have liked. He was still no nearer to formulating an opinion as to what to do on Saturday and the matter was becoming harder to bury, as evidenced by Katya's remarks. His instinct towards a pragmatic solution felt compromised by the sort of pride he had experienced in front of Katya when, instead of looking for a solution, he had let her believe that the game was not for throwing. This fool-hardy recklessness, though juvenile in inspiration, had nonetheless sprung from a true and utterly neglected part of his make-up. And it felt good to know that he had it in him, whether he really meant it or not.

Watching Tomsky leave the building from her hiding place, his tail, a tallish woman in her early forties with a large nose and a thatch of curly red hair, left her booth and walked up to the door of Katya Irena's office to begin her new assignment. Checking her watch to make sure she was not late, she knocked lightly on the door and walked in.

'Comrade Irena, Comrade Karoline Pavlova reporting for duty.'

For a moment Katya looked puzzled and distracted by this latest intrusion. 'Ah, of course, Pavlova, you're the replacement secretary, aren't you. I'm afraid you might find this new job rather boring compared to whatever you did last . . .'

'I was a school mistress in Leningrad, Comrade, and before that a student of philosophy . . .'

'Well, you won't find this anything like as satisfying as teaching or philosophy but . . .'

'I will, Comrade,' said the informant. 'Just show me to my desk and I'll begin.'

# Chapter Eight

Slovo had deliberately hung back and waited until Augustus Koba, dressing more slowly than usual, had gone before approaching Kasper, who was packing the last of his clothes into a sack that doubled as a kitbag.

'What is it, Slovo? There's something wrong, isn't there? You've been behaving strangely for the last few days. You're holding something in, I think.'

Slovo lowered his head like a naughty animal ready to be chastised. He was about to pour out his heart when he heard the booming voice of Copic rolling through the locker aisles. 'Combinations, my dear friends, combinations are what it's all about. Take a team like our illustrious rivals Dynamo. They must have – what is it? – five or six top-class forwards, but none that *combine* and play off each other like my Radek and Koba or Radek and Makhno or Radek and practically anyone can. Combinations are pairings born through skill and intuition. In my team you can combine anyone with anyone else – isn't that right, Kasper? Gentlemen of the French press, may I introduce you to Kasper and Slovo, goalkeeper and midfield playmaker respectively.'

The three French journalists, flushed with more vodka than they had ever been forced to drink in their lives, bowed and shook hands courteously, mindful of paying attention to the customs of this strange and exciting land.

'France, they're from France?' asked Slovo, his mind's eye already picturing his and Lotya's ascent of the Eiffel Tower. 'Do they have football teams in France too?'

'Yes,' replied one of the journalists in overly formal Russian, 'but whereas in your country soccer is a joyous affirmation of proletarian culture, in ours, I'm afraid, sport is little more than an opiate for the poor and oppressed, so burdened are they by the immediate misery of their thankless lives.'

'Quite right,' another journalist interjected. 'There is not one peasant or factory worker in France who would hesitate to drop his salaried life just to come and join you in the new life being built here . . .'

'From which we can only conclude life must be pretty awful in France.' Copic guffawed. For a second the foreign journalists looked confused but, sensing the irony, joined in the laughter, albeit somewhat nervously.

'Back to the football, gents, back to the fugging football. It's not just about combinations, it's also about *difference*. Take Koba, a completely instinctive striker who doesn't even know what the offside trap is – he pursues the ball wherever he finds it like an animal stalking its prey, and I wouldn't have it any other way. Radek, on the other hand – well, he's what you French might call a more cultivated player . . .'

Copic's voice trailed off as he, and his small procession of Frenchmen, made their way through the changing rooms and into the players' lounge. Slovo and Kasper were left alone once more.

'Do you really think it's worse in France than it is here?' asked Slovo.

'Governments are always killing their own people. I don't for one minute believe it's only ours that does it. Anyway, the workers are so poor in the West that they starve to death without the authorities even needing to kill them. That's what I heard anyway.'

Slovo eyeballed Kasper, causing him to break off eye contact. 'Come on, Kasper, you don't know any more than I do . . .'

'Then don't bother asking me such stupid questions. I was only trying to cheer you up, or perhaps you're looking for an excuse to be unhappy so you can get everyone to talk about you like they do Radek?'

'You know I'm not that type of person.'

'Then what are you so fret up about?'

'I have fallen in love.'

'Is that all, or is there something else too?'

'Isn't that enough?'

'That depends . . . well, go on, fill me in on it.'

'Her name is Lotya Pantya, she's a gymnast.'

'Grotsky's woman! Have you taken leave of your senses?' Kasper clenched his fingers into a fist and stabbed his chest. 'You may as well kill yourself if I've heard you rightly.'

'I think she loves me as well.'

'Do you mean to tell me you've actually been any-where near her?'

'Yes, of course I have.'

'But when did you get the chance?'

'This morning.'

'This morning! Please God tell me that you're jok-ing.'

Slovo said nothing; instead he waited patiently for his friend to overcome his incredulity and calm down.

'I mean it, I mean it, I've never heard of anything so fucking crazy in my life. You must want to die, Slovo, you must really want to leave this world and die.'

'Kasper, I think you're blowing things out of pro-portion . . .'

'Are you mad? If anything I'm understating the case. There're so many things that are fundamentally wrong about this that it's impossible to know where to begin. I mean, to start with, if we're to completely forget the dangers inherent in falling in love with an NKVD chief's floozy, there's the small matter of you not even knowing this girl, am I right?'

'It's true that I've only spoken to her once . . .'

'Then how the hell do you know that you love her?'

'That's what I wanted to talk to you about.'

'What?'

'You see, I agree with you, I know she's a dangerous person to fall in love with, which is why I need to be sure that I really do love her.'

'If it feels like you're in love, Slovo, it probably means that you are.'

'But how can you be sure that you are?'

'You can't.'

'Then how . . .'

'Look, the last thing I want to do after calling you a madman is convince you that you really are in love with this dangerous and quite probably equally mad girl . . .'

'Then I'll have to ask someone else . . .'

'No! Whatever you do, don't do that. Whatever you do, don't tell anyone else.'

'Then help me, Kasper, tell me how I can really *know* that I'm being led by something that *actually* exists.'

Kasper sighed and shook his head, his face a mask of exasperation. 'You're a blockhead, Slovo, a complete blockhead, but for what it's worth, and I'm not pretending it's worth much, this whole thing reminds me of the way I used to think about God. You see, I used to be a blockhead as well.'

'How do you mean?'

'When I was small I was a believer, just like everyone else in our village. We all were, and it wasn't only something we believed in, it was how we organised our lives and treated each other. Then one day the Communists came, confiscated the icons, turned the churches into schools and shot the priests. From that day on we were all told that God had ceased to exist, heaven was a lie and that we would all fall asleep for ever after we died. After that I started to feel a bit stupid about having believed in God for so long, but not just God, in all the other types of magic as well.

I began to look at things like sunsets and open fields and challenge God to do something to prove to me that he still existed. Give me some type of heavenly lift, or touch me in some way, perhaps make the sunset even more beautiful, I don't know, but anyway, the point is that in the end all of these things became empty for me. They stopped meaning anything.'

'What are you trying to say, that my love doesn't exist because God doesn't?'

'No, just the opposite, that both are articles of faith and are prevented by useless life-hating doubts. I should never have tried to make those sunsets stay still and "mean something"; I ought to have just followed their changing colours and shapes and watched them dissolve into the night sky. It's the same with love, it's not to be stopped and looked at, but something that should be followed and lived in the spirit of. I think you'd be mad to do this with Lotya but don't fool yourself – if you're even contemplating something so crazy then you're in love.'

'You see, I told you I was. When I'm thinking of her even time passes quickly. The next thing I know it's time to see her again.'

'What are you talking about? You told me you only met her once.'

'But before that we . . . we watched each other,' said Slovo mysteriously.

Kasper drew his cap over his eyes. 'That's another thing. You'll find that you'll never forget what she looks like between meetings if you're in love.'

'It's as if I'm looking at her now,' said Slovo.

Kasper followed his friend's eyes; they were staring at the white light pouring through the gap under the changing-room door. 'Come on, you can tell me about the rest later, if there is any more, that is.'

'There certainly is. We've made plans, you know.'

Kasper smiled benevolently, his earlier anger dissipating under the warmth of being treated as a confidant. It had been a long time since he had talked about love with anyone, and he was happy to find that he actually had something to say about it.

'So who have you been in love with before, Kasper?'

Kasper patted Slovo on the head, charmed by his friend's infantile simplicity. 'Too many people to tell you about, Slovo, too many people to tell you about in one go.'

As the two men walked out of the changing room, Slovo thought he could hear a song coming from deep within the hum of the boiler; it was singing, 'I love you, Slovo, I love you.'

Radek let Makhno out, closed the door and walked over to the window. The news that a party was to be held for him, that evening, in his flat, had been more than offset by what Makhno had had to say about Katya. Radek shook his head; the person he met in his dreams still loved him, and that image of Katya felt far more real and familiar to him than the one in the Ministry of Information who never wanted to see him again. If the dream was stronger than the reality of the woman, then he would continue to believe in the dream, since it was obvious that the real soul of Katya had left her body and was now living in a limbo land, able only to communicate to him through the deeper medium of sleep. It was in this region, rather than the one of football, that Radek felt his immediate future lay, and with this thought in mind he got back into bed and closed his eyes.

Spain and Russia smelt like two different countries. Josip knocked the frozen snot off his nose and brushed the icicles off his jacket. The softer ones crumbled like pine, the harder ones breaking off like rapier blades. In Spain the heat was always pushing objects downwards, so that the whole world felt as if it had shrunk by nightfall. One's own life grew larger as the significance the world reduced it to got smaller, allowing each man to live as the centre of his own universe. The geography was different in Russia; for one thing Josip felt little of the old insularity and the accompanying belief that his life might actually matter to anyone else. Here the wind was always pushing one upwards, away from other people and out into a glacial and empty nocturnal vastness. Josip had already learnt that he was not a creature who could survive in such an environment and had started to take this fatalism, and the cold weather he had discovered it in, personally. For if the heat smelt like home then the cold smelt of pain: pain and more cold.

At least there was his apartment, an outpost illuminated against the surrounding darkness and, for however short a time, safe from its worst effects. He pushed open the door and threw his sports bag over the fireguard. Muerta was sitting reading a book, looking unusually restful.

'What are you doing back here so early?' he asked, relieved to be speaking in Spanish again.

'Copic had some French visitors to show around and he gave me the rest of the day off.'

'Well, you can get up and make me some tea because I'm dying here, Muerta, really dying here. Every time the wind spits sleet into my face I ask why this is happening to me.'

Muerta laughed, but not without some concern. Although she was used to Josip complaining in small doses, it had grown into something of a character trait in the past few months, and one that only *she* had to put up with. She had noticed that he was careful not to do it around any of the Russians, and indeed cultivated the image of a detached man of the world when in their company. Russian had thus become the language he could act in, while Spanish was the language he chose to tell the truth through; a truth reserved for her ears only. She was careful, however, of judging him too harshly. She had lost a lot when they left Spain, but he had lost his family and, consequently, his entire life. And besides, unlike her he had never wanted to see the world.

'Will you be going to the party we're holding for Radek

tonight?' Josip asked, slightly embarrassed about being so open with his unhappiness.

'No, I don't think so. I hardly got any sleep last night and drinking all the time in this cold is bad for my skin. I smiled in the mirror today and saw little wrinkles either side of my lips.'

'You mean to say that you really won't come to a players' party with all those finely toned bottoms to pinch? This isn't the Muerta I know.'

'Oh well, the game's moved on.' She smiled. 'My world's changing quickly, and standing at a crowded party isn't going to help me understand it any better.'

'Tomsky will be there, you know. Are you so sure of yourself that you don't even want to consolidate your catch?'

'Tomsky *has* to be there whether he wants to or not. He has to attend anything to do with the players.'

'Except for team practice on cold days.' Josip laughed.

'Will there be lots of, you know, girls going?' Muerta asked, her new-found confidence lapsing slightly.

'Only "intimate acquaintances" and wives, no "new" friends or anyone else that can't be trusted to keep their mouths shut. No one wants their conversations repeated back to them by an interrogator in the Lubyanka.'

'But that still leaves a lot of wives and girlfriends . . .'

'I think it's safe to assume that they can be trusted not to denounce their husbands and boyfriends to the secret police . . .'

'No, that isn't what I meant. What I'm afraid of is that one of these wives will get drunk and try and get off with Tomsky. I've seen how randy these Russian women can get . . .'

'And Tomsky too, when he isn't trying to play the gentleman in front of you. You know, out of anyone I've ever known, even the Captain, he's the one who's best able to be different people at different times. And I don't mean that in a bad way, he's not false or deliberately deceitful, it's just that he's got a hell of a range on him. Which isn't something you notice when you first meet him.'

'I think I'm going to come along.'

'What about your skin?'

Muerta paused and looked in the mirror. In an instant her fear had become foolish to her and she started to laugh. Josip joined her, and for a few minutes they carried on chortling, the sound of each other's giggles occasioning more laughter.

'Why should anyone be afraid of being denounced to the secret police anyway? I mean, it's only a party, for God's sake.'

'I don't know,' said Josip through his chuckles. 'This country is as crazy as ours was during the last days of the war. It must be the Russian influence. But fuck it, you should come to the party anyway, and not just to spy on Tomsky but to be with him as well. A relationship's like life, you should enjoy it before you die.'

Muerta let her laughter settle on a smile. Josip, so familiar to her now, had once been her lover, but then so had an army captain who had disappeared in

Spain and countless other men. But in Josip's laughter, and now in Tomsky's, she could hear little bits of all of them, still laughing with her, still here. Unlike some women Muerta found this type of continuity reassuring and, with the warmth rising in her cheeks, she walked across the room to change for the party. It was only later that she remembered she had not said anything to Josip about Tomsky's fears for the game on Saturday, but by then she did not want to spoil either of their moods with thoughts of things that might never happen.

The party for Ivan Drago had started early at the Djugashvili club and the air was already thick with clouds of blue smoke. Large groups of NKVD men had congregated around the main bar and in the midst of them the odd Dynamo player could be seen fighting for air. The accumulated sound of their grunting chatter was deafening, and Grotsky was amused to see how their exaggeratedly aggressive behaviour, so normal at the training ground and the Lubyanka, turned heads and sent people hurrying towards the exits in this confined and 'neutral' space. Many of the Dynamo men were already rocking from side to side, and those who had been there all afternoon were starting to make their beds under the long banqueting tables at the end of the hall.

'It's the same with groups the world over, and group behaviour too,' he yelled over the din, ignoring Cretor's wounded silence (could he still be sulking after that verbal beating he had virtually asked for in the cell?). 'What's commonplace and run of the mill for members of the group can be infantile and slightly disturbing for anyone else, don't you agree? That's why all these good citizens who rely on our protection are leaving this place like flies, because they hate the sight of a secret policeman relaxing in the company he prefers the most; that of other secret policemen.'

Cretor nodded sullenly. He knew Grotsky too well to ignore him completely. His master's depressions and panic attacks tended to be followed by violence, and after the violence reflection. It was not uncommon for Cretor to be the recipient of all three stages and, as usual, he was heartily sick of the process.

'You see, take us communists,' Grotsky continued. 'Here we are, like Knights Templar in our own land, internal exiles surrounded by those who would crush us on one side and the enemy within on the other. Is it any wonder that we turn in on ourselves, distance ourselves from others and develop our own codes of behaviour that seem strange to them . . .' Grotsky gestured at an attendant for more vodka. 'But then, so what? The others? Who gives a fuck about the others, eh? We have our own work to do, and God help anyone, Russian or otherwise, who gets in our way. This has always been the way with our people, Cretor, us Bolsheviks, all or nothing. We were always in a minority, us right-thinking ones, having to drag the rest of them by their fucking bootstraps towards world revolution. Christ, if they had it their way we'd still have a parliament full of bourgeois bastards in neckties. We hate our enemies and they hate us. No one's come here for a tea party. We bring death or change, and if you don't like it . . .'

'. . . you can fuck off to England,' said Cretor, completing his boss's sentiment.

'Exactly. You can fuck off and take tea with the King of bloody England.'

They were sitting on a raised stage, just over the floor show, where a large and bored-looking Mongol was being fellated by an elderly whore. The stage was surrounded by open flame torches, Roman candles and hanging velvet drapes looted from St Basil's Cathedral. The medieval effect was compounded by the bearskin rugs and ox skulls heaped behind the mock throne that Grotsky sat upon. Cretor and Ivan Drago knelt either side of him on cushions, like junior minions in the court of Khan. This taste for gross overstatement was typical of an NKVD party, and everywhere browbeaten stewards, in the uniforms of Tsarist officers, exchanged sympathetic and knowing looks with each other, bound in their shared misfortune of having drawn the short straw to work this shift.

Grotsky drained the last of his mead and flung the yak-horn beaker over his shoulder with a flourish. 'The NKVD's changed since my day, Cretor, changed beyond recognition.' Grotsky gesticulated around the room and paused with his hand above Drago's head. 'Take a prize piece of meat like this one here; you think he could've made the Cheka under old Dzerzhinsky?

Would he hell! The party of Lenin wouldn't have let a brain-dead bollockhead like this through the front door, let alone into its vanguard.'

Drago nodded slavishly, pleased to assist in his own degeneration. 'He's here because he plays football and can beat the shit out of a kulak at the drop of a hat, but in the old days – remember them, Cretor? – in the old days you had to be in possession of balls of brass *and* a brain to be a secret policeman.'

Grotsky squeezed a pair of imaginary balls in his hand and grimaced, the vodka rising straight to his head as he did so. Cretor, sipping his drink more slowly than anyone else in the room, motioned for a steward to return Grotsky's tumbler from its landing place.

'*Us*,' mumbled Grotsky, losing the thread of his speech. 'Vodka?'

Drago stopped nodding for a moment and looked up as if to say something. Finding he had nothing to say, he got back down on his knees and opened his second bottle of vodka.

'You're right, boss, but what a long time ago that was, eh?' said Cretor with one eye on Drago. He knew full well that one bottle was usually the striker's limit.

'Damned right it was a long time ago,' spat Grotsky, warming to his theme again. 'In those days we were the fucking avant-garde, the cutting edge who only accepted the best into our ranks. *Us*, the first generation of secret policemen, it was us who first smoked French fags and read fucking Mayakovsky long before Trotsky "discovered" him in *Literature and Revolution* . . .'

'Careful, Klimt, that's a banned work . . .'

'Don't you "careful" me. Who do you think helped our recluse in the Kremlin to ban it, eh? Yagoda? Beria? Or one of those other cowardly fucks from Leningrad? Did they fuck! *I* was the one the Boss would call for in the old days, I was the one who would talk to him until it grew light . . .'

'Come on, Klimt, we don't want to talk theory all night, like a couple of dickless intellectuals.'

Grotsky paused. There was something in what his assistant had said. There were safer things to talk about when drunk.

Cretor smiled hopefully and continued, 'You've said it yourself on many occasions, the one thing this country has too much of is intellectuals who don't know shit about how things really work. Take our own Bukharin, for instance – he can't even keep up with reality, let alone advise the rest of us on theory . . .'

'You're right, dammit, Cretor, you're right. So let's have no more of that talk, no, no more speaking of theory in my presence,' shouted Grotsky, addressing the floor show beneath him. 'Speak only of fucking and cunts. Speak only of the way ahead,' he screamed at the roaring crowd of drunk secret policemen.

'Fucking and cunts,' yelled the sycophantic Gorfsky from the assembled throng. 'I'll drink to those!' Stumbling into a table of prostitutes, the obese lech lowered his trousers and began to pull at his genitalia. 'That's one hundred per cent Gorfsky, my good ladies, one hundred per cent good communist Russian.'

From his place on the stage Grotsky shook his head. He had never had much affection for his first-team coach, and he saw no reason to pretend otherwise now. 'Gorfsky, this isn't your birthday, it's Drago's. He scores goals, you kiss arses. Raise your game or put it away, you whore's melt.'

The table of prostitutes started to laugh and Gorfsky felt his member shrink in his hand. Acting quickly, he turned his attention to the hapless Mongol, who was still being serviced, somewhat more slowly than before, by his elderly companion. 'Faster, you bastard! Come over her face!'

The Mongol looked over apologetically and the terrified woman set about her task with a reinvigorated sense of purpose. All of which was not enough for Gorfsky, who, aware that the eyes of the room were on him, shouted more unfriendly encouragement at the struggling pair.

Discreetly, but pre-empting what would occur next, disgusted stewards and wine waiters backed off towards the exits, shaking their heads, whilst excited NKVD men took their places surrounding the stage.

'Show them some mercy, Gorfsky. How much faster do you want them to go?' called Cretor from the podium, determined to strike a reasonable note amidst the mayhem.

'Damn you, Genghis,' spluttered Gorfsky, any bonhomie now entirely absent from his voice. Using all the strength his stubby little arms could muster, he picked up a burning torch and hurled it contemptuously at the floor show. Though falling some way short of its target, the flame succeeded in catching the fur rug upon which the unhappy couple were performing and, within seconds, a small line of fire spread over the bearskin, towards Grotsky's podium. Waitresses and barmen quickly hurried away from the trajectory of the advancing fire, as behind them chairs and tables were abandoned and drapes burned. Sensing some fun, the drunkest of the NKVD men began to hurl beakers, cucumbers and legs of meat at the foot of the stage, followed by bottles, coins and chairs. The whore, sensing her hair singe from the heat, abandoned her task and fled towards the exit. The unfortunate Mongol, trying desperately to avoid the ensuing flames and missiles, continued to masturbate furiously, keen not to spoil the 'entertainment', and also to save his life.

'No one wants to see a naked Chinky jack himself off,' yelled Gorfsky in an attempt to imitate the wit of his master, Grotsky. 'Who the hell do you think we are, a bunch of bloody perverts?'

The Mongol looked up to the podium for instructions, but before he could receive any he was forced to dive for cover as Gorfsky drew his revolver, aimed at the man's crotch and fired. Missing entirely, the bullet travelled through a burning curtain, killing a young cloakroom attendant who had arrived from Vladivostock that morning.

The fire, by now, had reached the roof, and the first beams were creaking under the strain of the heat. Everywhere prostitutes were running from table to table, filling their hands and pockets with food and leftover cutlery. Even a few of those who had passed out were now gently stirring to life to see what the commotion was all about, only to be trampled in the rush to the exits. In the middle of the room, still on the raised stage, stood Grotsky, oblivious to the ensuing panic, the heat from the flames and the collapsing beams. Instead he appeared to be malevolently bored, neither satisfied nor distracted by the sequence of disasters playing out under his nose. Propped up behind him leered Cretor, safe as long as he was under his master's protection, an oafish grin spreading across his face as he watched the Mongol, now being strangled by the paralytic Drago, beg for his life.

'Perhaps we ought to go too, Klimt. There's no sense in hanging around until the fire brigade get here. It'll just mean more paperwork.'

'Relax,' muttered Grotsky over the creak of the breaking woodwork. 'You don't need to worry about this building, it's got strong foundations. They're made of the same stuff as we are; stone.'

Smiling, he beckoned to a young tart who was busy emptying her sleeping escort's pockets of all the valuables she could carry. Ignoring the monster on the podium, the girl stuffed the last of the booty down her front and joined the queue flocking to leave the burning building.

The three men loitering by the mahogany staircase looked like secret policemen and Tomsky brushed past them without saying hello. Usually their presence would have worried him, because where there were police there were also arrests, but he had lived among their kind long enough to know that it wasn't him they were after tonight. Ignoring them, he walked up to Radek's flat and knocked loudly. The door was opened by an open-eyed but slight woman in a Ukrainian nightshirt who he recognised as Makhno's sister Vera. Without wasting any time on greetings he hurried in and closed the door behind him. All three secret policemen watched the door close and, one after another, shrugged in a way that indicated they had more serious things to do than watch Tomsky go to a party.

'I trailed him for a whole year after he came back from America, but I never got anything on him. That was what you needed in the old days, actual information on your suspects,' said the leader of the group, a large man in a pea-green raincoat. 'Yeah, all our Tomsky did all day was visit young women, which is nice work if you can get it.'

The youngest of the policemen laughed loudly; he had been blackmailed into joining the NKVD after being caught in bed with Guy Hubbard, the English journalist. His original plan had been to join the Russian State Theatre and become an actor, but circumstances had forced him to inform on all his former colleagues, and he was now reconciled to the lonely life of an NKVD man. 'What I'd give to have a woman here now,' he said bluffly. 'I haven't had a piece of arse in weeks.'

The older man nodded sympathetically; he did not know his junior colleague's secret. 'I know what you're going through. It was just our luck to pull the short straw and draw duty on the night of Drago's damned birthday.'

'The lucky bastards,' said the third man, a former wrestler and the simplest of the three. 'I heard Grotsky's laid on a real treat for them, a live show, thousands of tarts, the whole bloody caboodle . . .'

'Well, let's get a move on and maybe we'll catch the end of it' said the man in the pea-green raincoat. 'Lunacharsky, you watch the corridor. Make sure you keep an eye on any of those Spartak morons coming in and out of the party; it'd be bloody awkward if any of them got involved. The last thing we need now is a situation on our hands.'

'Kropotkin,' he said, pointing at the former actor, 'you come with me.'

Both men marched briskly to the end of the corridor, stopping at the last apartment before the fire escape.

'Have you got your pistol with you?'

'Of course.'

'Is the safety catch off and have you loaded the thing? We can't afford any mistakes.'

'Yes.'

'Good, because we don't want to be taking any chances tonight. I've seen that happen too many times before.'

The younger man sighed inwardly. It was absolutely typical of his boss to build up and overestimate the dangers of their work; in truth there was no risk at all in arresting an elderly historian for a crime he had yet to confess to.

'Right, then, let's get on and do what we're paid to do,' said the man in the overcoat. Stepping back, self-importantly, he kicked open the flimsy door with ease and surprised the victim, just as he was about to tell his wife of fifty years how much he still loved her.

'Ivan Vyshinsky, I presume you know who we are, and what we are here for.'

'Yes,' said the old man, and, to the policeman's surprise, added, 'Just let me get my things.'

Tomsky looked down at the table overflowing with food. There was a plate of mutton, two chickens, wheat gruel with butter, dried cherries and salted melon. There was also something touching about the way the food had been had arranged which demonstrated a type of care rarely seen at a players' party.

'Did you get all this together?' Tomsky asked Vera Makhno, who had followed him over from the door-way.

'I did, yes.'

'It was a very sweet thing for you to do,' said Tomsky, helping himself to a cherry, before adding, 'I really mean it.'

Vera blushed slightly. She had heard that Tomsky had been behaving oddly over the past few days, but she had never heard him talk to her this tenderly before.

'Radek needed cheering up. It was nothing. I'd do it for any one of them.'

'Speaking of the boy wonder, where is the guest of honour?'

'Um, in the bath, actually.'

Tomsky looked at his watch. It had just gone nine. 'The bath? How the hell did he get in there so quickly? Even at this football club we obey certain traditions of restraint.'

'He was so touched, and surprised, when we all started arriving that he downed most of the first cask of beer we opened, mixed it with some brandy Koba bought him . . .'

'Brandy? Isn't that what NKVD men drink?'

Vera rolled her eyes knowingly. '. . . and sank the lot in one go. Then he burst into tears and told us what grand friends we all were and how happy he was to have us here. And he carried on like that until he passed out in the bath about ten minutes ago.'

Tomsky looked around the room. 'Well, at least it doesn't look as though the tears were infectious. There must be at least thirty people crammed in here.'

Vera also looked around the room, coyly, as if a thought had only just occurred to her. 'And I suppose you're wondering if that Spanish girl is one of them. Well, she is. She's over there with my brother and Guardiola.'

Tomsky resisted the urge to barge straight over and leave Vera so obviously. 'Why don't you have a crack at Josip? He's a handsome-looking man and seems like he knows how to treat women well. He's probably as lonely as hell too. I don't mean to be crude or patronising, I just think that you'd both benefit from each other, that's all.'

Vera laughed filthily. 'No, I don't think he's the one for me. He's very – how can I put it? – male . . . I might try my luck later, I suppose. Anyway, go on, go to your Spanish hussy, I can tell you're already tired of talking to me.'

With this Vera disappeared behind the broad shoulders of Kasper and into the arms of her lover, Lilly Beli, a nutritionist at the children's hospital.

Avoiding the mass of swinging elbows and food-filled hands, Tomsky circumnavigated his way to the corner where Muerta was already awaiting him. Beside her stood Josip, deep in conversation with Makhno, who, like his sister, was dressed in a faded Ukrainian garment.

'What's that you're wearing, skinny?' said Tomsky, as he bundled his way between the two men.

'The rags my mother was shot in after eating the bark off a fir tree,' said Makhno emotionlessly.

The silence was broken by loud four-way laughter.

'She must have been very hungry,' said Muerta.

'She was. Starving, in fact. Like the rest of the Ukraine that year.'

Tomsky smiled and said to Muerta, 'Makhno likes to shock us with these little vignettes. Which is not to say they're not true, of course, just that the Ukraine isn't the only part of the country to have gone without food or to have suffered a little.'

'When he puts on his elegant airs, that is to say when there's a girl around, Tomsky can have quite a way with understatement. But I let it go,' said Makhno, pursing his lips mournfully. 'I always let it go.'

'Why's that? From what I've seen you seem to like a good one-two,' said Muerta, happy to be around so many men, and happy to listen to them spar in a way that fascinated her.

'Because despite his many and peculiar faults, not least his laziness, personal vanity and tactlessness, Tomsky is one of the few people in this country whom I can trust. By which I mean that when I play that game of going through my circle of friends and trying to work out which of them is an informer or spy, Tomsky's name is one that never comes up.'

'You must be flattered,' said Muerta, turning to Tomsky.

'I must say I am. It's very kind of the old partisan to be so free and easy with his compliments for once and, for what it's worth, the feeling is reciprocated. He's right as well. You either stop meeting people altogether, learn to lie or talk about things that you know you won't lie about – which, of course, rules most things out – or you take the leap of faith and work out who you can trust. By my estimation I'd say that most of our squad is good in this respect, but, as of this afternoon, I've been given a couple of nasty surprises. Though perhaps a shrew like our Makhno here wouldn't have been quite so surprised.'

'No.' Muerta laughed, as if she were taking part in the first stage of some wonderful game. 'I bet that the shrew Makhno was on to them months ago!'

Makhno smiled. 'I cannot tell a lie. I think I know one of the men you're talking about.' And he tilted his head to one side. Tomsky, Muerta and Josip followed his eyes across the room. They were aimed at Augustus Koba, the giant centre-forward, who was now on all fours with his head up the skirt of a tall, and very thin, former countess. Nothing about his manner suggested that he suspected he was the subject of their conversation.

'We should talk about this later, along with an even bigger problem that you may have already heard about as well,' said Tomsky.

Makhno nodded sagely and pulled Josip by the arm. 'Come on, we need to start drinking properly. Being with these two is affecting my digestion.'

Josip allowed himself to be dragged through the packed room, and into an adjoining cubby-hole heaped full of old football magazines. Makhno sat himself down on a stack and offered Josip a hip flask. The Catalan accepted cautiously. 'I'm not used to your rock fuel yet. Where I come from alcohol usually h     in it.'

     smiled, flashing his teeth mischievously.
     unds like a soft place. No wonder you
     o during the Civil War. I don't know,

you can speak our language perfectly but you balk at our alcohol . . .'

'I think we got by pretty well before you Russians came to our "assistance".' Josip knocked the flask back, swallowed the liquid and frowned. 'That was fucking awful.'

'Believe me, that was nothing. You've got it all still to look forward to.'

Josip touched his stomach. His intestines felt as if they were on fire. 'And am I right in thinking that this delicacy has been laid on to prepare me for the conversation you warned me about last night?' he asked.

'You think right,' Makhno replied, 'though I'm sorry we couldn't have made the conference room more salubrious.'

'Don't worry,' Josip quipped back, 'it's a nice area and with the number of cops around here I'm unlikely to be raped on my way home.'

Makhno wheezed and patted his chest. 'Never take anything for granted.' He coughed again. 'I'm going to have to give cigarettes up. Whenever I smoke a box and play the next day my chest starts to hurt.'

'That's just age. So tell me, it was you who put that note under my door inviting me to the "émigré meeting", wasn't it?'

'Yes, it was. My sister's idea actually, the bit about the émigré meeting, but I went along with it.'

'Why take me there at all?'

'Because I thought you might be missing open political debate since you arrived in this country.'

'You're joking, aren't you?'

'Well, why did you think you were invited? And why, since we're on the subject of questions, do you think we're talking now?'

'I don't know but I certainly don't think it's because you're a lonely old Ukrainian exile who misses political conversations since your "revolution" became a police state.'

'Then why?'

'Because you want me to join some secret underground terrorist cell that you're a part of. Or perhaps you've learnt something about my background and decided the best place for me to stand is shoulder to shoulder with you in your fight, for whatever it is you think we both stand for.'

Makhno laughed. 'And you're angry because you think I don't realise that you've given up politics?'

'Yeah, something like that.'

'Well, you're wrong, it's nothing like that.'

'Are you trying to tell me that you come from a race of conspirators, but don't have a plan of action?'

'I can see that you really were expecting one.' Makhno laughed.

'To go to the risk of having meetings, but not any plans, seems crazy to me. At the very least I thought you would ask me to kill Grotsky as part of the initiation into your little band. And if not murder, then an attempt to sabotage the system in some other way.'

'You Spanish are all assassination crazy. And you worry too much as well. The system? You're right, I hate it and I think it's shit but that doesn't mean I need to kill it, any more than you need to kill Grotsky. You see, once the system has run out of people to kill, it'll kill itself. And it's the same with Grotsky and even the Boss. By the time he's finished killing he'll be the only one of those bastards left alive, and he'll die alone. As for anyone who outlasts him, well, they'll already be dead, dead because of the mediocrity they fell into just to survive.'

Josip did not know whether to believe what he was hearing, let alone understand it. Was it possible that Makhno was the ultimate agent provocateur, hired by the secret police to bring Josip's past into the open and thus unmask him as a foreign agent of Spanish Fascism? He had heard of such things happening before. And yet Josip already knew and liked Makhno, and his instincts told him the man was exactly what he seemed to be; a dangerous but genuine madman.

'So this is what you want to chat to me about? A dissection of the Soviet system according to one Nestor Makhno? I'm sorry if I seem slow on the uptake but I don't know where this is going or what you're asking me to do.'

'I want to tell you to stop worrying and to learn to live amongst all this. Things may not be perfect but the good stuff is already here with us.' Makhno pointed to the swarm of bodies in the adjoining room. 'Parties like this, your friend and mine falling in love with each other, or us beating Dynamo this weekend. We may be living in a vast slave camp but look at all this.' He waved his hand. 'I'm not just talking about pockets of resistance, I'm talking about a whole line of life and energy that they can never touch. So stop worrying. I know you try and play it cool but I've watched you sweat even more than the rest of us. You've been that way ever since you came here, I've seen it on your face, and it's even affected your team performances and game . . .'

'I haven't been *that* worried,' protested Josip.

'Sure, things could be better,' Makhno carried on, ignoring him, 'but stop making yourself sick about it. If we die we die, but in the end the truth will out and good will win . . .' He paused, took another swig from his hip flask and smiled somewhat hysterically. 'This may be the arse-end of nowhere, as far as you're concerned, but it doesn't stop each minute from still being a miracle.'

Josip did not know whether this was inspired or madness. 'I think I'm beginning to understand . . .' he lied.

'What we're playing is the ultimate waiting game,' Makhno continued. 'In a way it's a bit like feeling superior to a herd of animals – there's no point in offending any of them, just hold back and remain on the ball. Then when the time comes you'll be ready, and if it never does, at least you'll have known you weren't one of those stupid fools who stood in line, a chamber pot in one hand and Stalin's collected works in the other.'

'In Spain we used to call people like you anarchists.'

Ignoring Josip, Makhno went on, 'Tonight or tomorrow you'll be asked whether you want to throw the game against Dynamo this weekend. I don't know who will ask you but it will probably be Tomsky. He'll want you to say no, but he won't show it. Think carefully before you answer but . . .'

'. . . but who wants to live for ever,' said Josip.

Makhno laughed quietly and punched Josip on the shoulder. 'You're a good man, Guardiola, a good man. I think you're starting to get it . . .' His compliment was interrupted by a loud and fierce banging on the door.

'That doesn't sound too friendly,' said Josip, who, for reasons he could not entirely fathom, was pleased to find that, for the first time since he had arrived in Russia, he was not scared by the sound of violent knocking, or even the thought of having to refuse to throw the game to retain Makhno's respect.

'Turn down that gramophone,' ordered Tomsky as he pushed his way through the crowd. 'And get away from the door.'

Unlike Muerta, who was afraid that her time had come now that she wanted to enjoy it the most, Tomsky was unafraid. It was not like the secret police to arrest a whole party of people, or even a few people from such a large party.

Carefully, and without rushing, he pulled open the door. Standing on the other side of it was a heavily inebriated Copic, still dressed in his shiny red-and-white Spartak tracksuit.

'Hello, boss,' said Tomsky, 'this is a nice surprise.'

Ignoring him, Copic barged past and staggered straight towards the table loaded with vodka.

'Thought you could keep Copic out of his own boy's party,' he muttered at no one in particular. 'Well, we'll show those bastards, won't we, my lad?'

'Good of you to turn up, boss. We don't see too much of you at players' events,' said Kasper amicably, as he poured Copic a drink.

'That's because it's important to keep a distance from clowns like you or else you'll start to take liberties,' said Copic, rocking from foot to foot like a sailor in a storm. 'Ran out of booze in the office and needed some more. If I didn't you wouldn't have seen me here for dust. Old Copic's a mean old snow fox who does his boozing alone. You would too if you had my problems . . . and my decisions to make.'

'Even so, it's good to see you, boss. You should come out with us more often.'

Copic spat out his drink and stumbled into Vera Makhno, who was midway through a passionate embrace with Lilly Beli.

Copic stared at her, his face almost resting on her shoulders. Patiently she stared back, her expression far less troubled than his own, but no less intense in its purpose. At last he said, 'Has anyone ever told you, you look like a boy?'

Vera smiled and gently pushed his face away. Copic stumbled back a few paces, fell into the wall, keeled over and, on hitting the ground, passed out.

Kasper looked down at him with concern. 'I hope he's all right for practice in the morning,' he said.

'What are you worrying about him for?' said Vera. 'He's as tough as snakeskin.'

'I wouldn't normally, it's just these pills Koba gave me. He says a friend of his in the organs uses them as a truth drug. I thought I'd take a few to relax, but since they've kicked in I can't stop worrying about people.'

'You mean you're becoming paranoid?'

'No, just the opposite. I want everyone to be okay and out of harm's way . . .'

Vera started to giggle.

'. . . and out of the way of anything that could bring harm to them.'

'That sounds quite frightening. I hope you don't think that you need to worry about me?'

'I'm worrying about everyone but mainly . . .' Kasper stopped himself. The last thing he wished to do was blurt out Slovo's ridiculous plan to anyone, even Vera. It was because of this that he had taken the evil pills in the first place. And even if he did tell the truth, which was a difficult thing not to do when in the grip of a truth drug, who would believe that he was panicking because his flatmate intended to kill the chief of secret police and escape across the border with his mistress?

Lilly, Vera's girlfriend, took Kasper's shaking wrist and held it in between her thumb and forefinger. 'Are you all right? Your pulse is racing like you've just completed a marathon.'

'What was it that you were trying to say, Kasper?' said Vera, her tone becoming slightly more serious.

Kasper realised that if he opened his mouth he would only be able to tell the truth. No kind of tactical evasion or white lie was possible. Just within earshot he could hear Koba, who had also taken a pill, barking lustfully at the ex-countess, thus demonstrating that he was not the only man in the room for whom the pills were working. How he wished for a response as simple as Koba's, instead of the mental hell that was now descending upon him. He could feel the sweat on his back turn cold. He knew he would have to keep his lips sealed but his head was already spinning with the desire to talk. He was saved, momentarily at least, by the sudden intervention of Slovo, who had bounded over the moment he saw the colour leave his friend's cheeks.

'He'll be okay,' he said to Lilly. 'He's crazy mixing these pills with vodka.'

'Then why did he?' asked Vera.

'You know what he's like, he's after those mystical visions of his. Here, let me get him to a window.'

Slovo pulled Kasper away from the two women and on to the ledge of the solitary, oval-shaped bay window. 'What's the matter with you, Kasper, what are you playing at and why aren't you saying anything?'

Kasper felt his mouth bend under the pressure to speak, but no words were coming through. It wasn't that his urge to speak had passed; it was just that he was physically no longer able to. And yet his head was alive with words, conversations and voices, all of them urging him to tell the 'truth', though which truth this was, he was no longer sure.

'Kasper, you're starting to worry me. Say something, will you?'

'I'll . . . I'll not betray you, my friend,' Kasper blurted through his teeth.

'I don't understand. Why should you?'

Kasper tried to open his mouth again. The colour was returning to his cheeks but only because he was glowing bright red with embarrassment and frustration. What he was trying to say was simple enough but the discrepancy between his speech and the speed of his thoughts was making the production of words impossible. He felt absolutely fucked, but saying this would make things sound simpler than they were.

'You're not still worried about my plan, are you? I knew I shouldn't have told you. I ought to have guessed that there's no way you'd ever be able to understand something like this.'

Kasper frowned; his friend was misrepresenting him. He understood why Slovo and Lotya had hatched their plan; it was just that they had no idea what it would mean to actually make it happen, and what the consequences of this would be. But all this felt like too much for a single voice to express, especially as Kasper knew that he would have to say it all at once, to make any kind of impact on Slovo at all. Besides, he was afraid that his description of the consequences of Slovo's plan would replace the brute reality of what it would be like to experience it, thus lessening the force of his warning.

'I know you think I don't know what I'm doing, but what you have to see is . . .'

'No, I mean yes, I *do* know what you're doing, but I . . .'

Kasper stopped mid-sentence. His words were sounding as if they belonged to someone else, and he no longer recognised the grain of his own voice. Everything was passing before him too quickly and, as he stared at Slovo's puzzled face, he realised that he had forgotten what he was trying to say.

'Is it these pills you got off Koba or are you going mad on me?'

Kasper smiled helplessly, desperately trying to remember what the conversation was all about. His head was stubbornly holding out on him, preventing him from understanding a thought without then forgetting ten others, or grasping one without losing track of where the last had come from.

'Shit, Slovo, I feel gone, completely gone . . .'

'How do you mean? Like when you've drunk too much vodka?'

'Yes, except I'm completely aware of what's happening to me, I mean, what I'm thinking . . .'

'Then why aren't you talking properly?'

'Because I . . .' Kasper gulped noiselessly; what the hell was 'I', and what did it mean? 'What I mean is . . .' he continued, playing for time.

'What *do* you mean, you chump?'

'I can't remember,' Kasper spluttered. 'I mean, what are you asking me? Do you mean what do I mean by "mean"?'

'Are you taking the piss?'

'No, you said "I" mean. Didn't you?'

Slovo shook his head. 'What the fuck's the matter with you? I thought these pills were meant to make you tell the truth, but all you're doing is stringing the needle like a complete tithead. Come on, you're usually the most concise fellow I know.'

Kasper rubbed his eyes. His head was doubling in on itself with ever-greater ferocity, as his thoughts turned over a million and one possible meanings for the expression 'tithead'. It was no good even trying to talk to Slovo now, he was too far away from him, and it felt as though they would never understand each other again. Light years had passed since he had last said anything, and he had been through too much in that time ever to transmit its essence to anyone else, let alone a reckless buffoon like Slovo. Never in his life had he realised how many feelings 'tithead' could be associated with, or how many different contexts it worked in, each one hitting him like the discovery of a new galaxy, each with its own unique form of life and moral system. The simple phrase seemed vast to him in scope, and infinite in content. It was as if he had reached up for a tin, but ended up bringing the whole shelf down on his head – a feeling at once so peaceful and enlightening that Kasper was afraid that he might be deceiving himself; could anything really be this beautiful?

Slovo returned from the bar with a mug in his hand. 'Here, get some of this down you, you look like you're constipated.' He smiled, pleased that his friend's anxious frowning had been replaced by an idiotic grin.

Kasper accepted the mug gratefully and downed its contents in one; the whole room seemed enveloped in a sea of smiles, as wave after wave drifted up, past and through him. Everything from the canoe paddles to the old football magazines, from Vera's stockings to Slovo's shaved head emanated warmth, life and memory . . .

'Slovo.'

'Yes . . . ?'

'You don't need to worry, it'll all be all right, I can see how it all fits together now, and I want you to know that you'll be all right. I want you to know that,' he repeated, squeezing Slovo's hand.

'Thank you, Kasper,' said Slovo, abashed but also relieved at his friend's sudden return to clarity. 'It means a lot to me to know that you think I'm doing the right thing.'

'I do because I realise that there isn't any force in the world that can stop you from doing it,' Kasper intoned, his eyes shining in the flickering candlelight.

'You're right,' said Slovo, 'you're right. There's nothing that'll stop me.'

'Christ, what's that?'

The room shook with the force of knocking on the door for the second time that night. This time, unlike the last, a hushed silence spread across the packed group of revellers. The odds game decreed that this sort of noise would, sooner or later, have to be the work of the secret police. Gingerly Tomsky edged towards the door and, this time expecting the worst, flung it open.

'Oh my fucking God.'

'Evening, Tomsky, you wicked old forbidden fruit you,' Hubbard exclaimed, his words drowned in the stink of cherry schnapps. 'Thought I might perhaps come along and give that centre-half of yours a good plating.'

Hubbard was dressed in an ill-fitting sequined frock, a university scarf and bright orange snow boots.

'This may sound quite an arbitrary question in the circumstances, Guy, but did you walk here dressed like that?'

'Oh, let me in, you fashion-conscious bitch, I'm feeling as horny as an ox and if I don't bury my itch in the next five minutes expect custard to fly indiscriminately.'

'Be my guest,' said Tomsky. 'Slovo, the boy you're looking for, he's over there by that window. But be gentle with him, he's not seen much of the horrors of this world.'

'Gentle be damned! Since when did young boys like "gentle"? As usual you're hopelessly out of your depth, Tomsky! Now where is he? Let me at the randy little calf!'

Slovo, who had just achieved a state of Zen-like serenity with Kasper, stared at the advancing figure of

Hubbard with complete bewilderment. He looked over at Tomsky, who shrugged his shoulders apologetically and smiled.

'What was all that noise about?' said Kasper, returning to the world of events again.

'It was him,' Slovo stuttered, and pointed at the leering Hubbard, who had managed to grope his way through the crowd and was now standing before him, hands on hips and legs astride; a perfect vision of British strangeness.

'Now, my little brass monkey, shall we wonder like the Greeks, if you'll pardon the pun, or would you rather we got on and did what monkeys do?'

Aghast and confused, Slovo dropped his drink and turned to Kasper for help. Unfortunately for him, Kasper had done exactly the same thing to someone else, and was now in Vera's arms blubbering about gross hallucinations. Panicking, and not knowing what else to do, Slovo stepped up to Hubbard and, as lightly as he could, punched him in the face. There was the sickening crack of a bone breaking followed by a cuckoo-like whimper. From his place on the floor Hubbard cackled through a mouthful of blood, 'Tomsky, you cunning wretch, you didn't tell me he was such a butch little bugger.'

'I knew you'd prefer finding out for yourself,' said Tomsky, helping Hubbard up off the floor.

'It's been an absolute pleasure so far, but where's the filthy little tease run off to? I almost had the taste of salt in my mouth back there.'

'Ha,' snorted an ugly little man with a beard, who neither Hubbard or Tomsky had ever met before, 'you play parlour games like a family of fat weasels while Rome burns!'

'Who are you?' asked Tomsky.

'Never you mind who I am, you cheeky little cock, though I'm a poet for your information, a fusion between this world and the next, past, future and time present.'

'Well, don't just stand there looking ugly, give us some bloody poetry, you windy bastard,' said Hubbard.

'Ha! I'll give you poetry, it's a fact I will!' said the little man, who Tomsky now suspected of being at the very least demented. 'We live,' he practically yelled, 'deaf to the land beneath us, ten steps away no one hears our speeches, *All we hear is the Kremlin Crag dweller, the murderer and peasant slayer . . .*'

'The roof!' someone shouted. 'Let's all go on to the roof!'

'A splendid idea,' roared Copic, who had been roused from his slumber, 'a fucking splendid idea!'

Muerta grabbed Tomsky's arm. 'Come on, let's go!'

The room was already half empty by the time the poet finished his recital. 'Come on, Daddy,' Vera said to him, 'it's time to go.'

'What are we doing up here?' mumbled Copic pitifully. 'It's fucking freezing.'

'Are you mad?' giggled Muerta. 'It's absolutely beautiful!'

Tomsky could see it both ways. The view from Radek's roof *was* beautiful, but it was also fucking freezing.

'I've never seen my pistol shrivel to such a manageable size,' bawled Hubbard as he urinated off the side of the building, 'or my piss turn to ice before. You've got to be a tough old bird to fly out here, what?' He cackled.

Twitching nervously, Slovo had to restrain himself from pushing the unfortunate Englishman off the building and down on to the clanking tram tracks below. Gently, Lilly Beli squeezed his hand. 'I've never liked boys before but I think you're different, aren't you?'

Slovo gulped down his drink and turned red. Several years of being ignored had left him spectacularly ill prepared for all the attention he was receiving tonight. But she was right; he was not like others.

'I tell you, this view might be a turn-on for artists, lovers and other part-timers, but I'm on my way downstairs. It's too cold to even breathe up here,' Copic moaned.

'Does someone want to help the boss downstairs? He's not looking too steady on his feet,' said Tomsky.

'Damn your charity,' Copic snapped, his voice flitting between anger and pastiche. 'You mark my words,' he continued, turning towards Muerta, 'it's all fresh air and love for you up here, but don't you make the mistake I did; don't get too used to life or any of the things in it. Here we are, spinning around on this lump of granite, and we think we're safe ... *safe*.' Copic almost spat out the word.

'But we're not, are we, boss?' said Tomsky as he put his scarf around Copic's neck.

'For God's sake, of course we're not, Tomsky,' said Copic, his small eyes burning with the fervour of a saint. 'We've never been in more danger in our lives. Do you understand what will happen to us if we go out and win on Saturday? They'll take all of this' – Copic waved his arm round in a circle, his feet only just keeping their balance on the treacherous surface – 'away from us, and leave us with that.' He pointed at the dark remains of a coal chute.

'Easy, boss.'

'This decision,' Copic continued, his voice shaking with emotion, 'this decision is tearing me apart.'

Tomsky looked at Muerta, who looked away.

Copic nodded unhappily and took Tomsky's hand. 'You see, she knows, Tomsky, she can see that the next stop for us is capitulation or death.'

'For God's sake, boss, you're running with it ...'

'I don't need your reassurance, I know I'm on my way to meet them now ...'

'Meet who?'

'My sons. My sons in heaven with their mother.'

'You're as drunk as a lord. You know as well as I do that your sons aren't dead.'

'I told you, no more lies!' shouted Copic. 'I've had it with 'em, had it with all lies and liars.'

'Can someone give me a hand with him?' called

Tomsky, catching Copic by the arm and taking his vodka away from him. 'Here, let me tie your scarf back on.'

Copic stood still and let Tomsky knot the scarf. 'I want you to know something,' he said.

'What?'

'I love you.'

'And I love you, Copic.'

With a thundering clang, the clock on the Spassky Tower chimed midnight, and with it the sound of 'The Internationale' could be heard, drifting across the empty Kremlin forecourt, past the electric floodlights at the foot of the statue of Lenin, and on through the burning remains of the Djugashvili club, right up to the group huddled together on the roof.

'I don't know whether to cry or to join in,' said Hubbard as he staggered towards the fire escape, his narrow blue eyes glazing over. 'It reminds me of Cambridge, the old debating society, home . . .'

'It reminds me of being a young communist 'Pioneer' and having to sing it every time we went camping. God, I hated that uniform,' said Kasper in a faraway voice.

'I bet you looked quite cute in shorts,' said Muerta, wrapping herself in Tomsky's jacket.

'Cute?' said Kasper. 'Cute? . . . It reminds me of . . .' His voice trailed off as his mind filled up with images of his childhood and other related catastrophes.

A cold gust of wind blew over the roof, scattering snowflakes in every direction. The party began to break up as couples, not wanting the cold to catch up with them, raced each other over the slippery ice to the stairway. At their front was Augustus Koba and his countess, her face a picture of blissful contentment, his mottled in a troubled frown.

'I suspect those pills must be wearing off now,' said Vera, following them on to the fire escape.

Koba winced and closed his eyes.

'I hate it when a party comes to an end too, my dear,' said the countess, with her hand on his thickset neck.

Koba, preferring not to look at Vera, whimpered to himself and continued down the stairs, his large frame looking unusually small in the dark light.

Not joining them, Kasper looked up to the heavens in the hope that nature would help absorb his troubled and overactive mind. Instead he saw something he was not expecting. Right above him, moving faster than any plane he had ever seen, was a falling constellation of shooting stars, lighting up the sky like a giant arc.

'Did you see it?'

'Fuck me, I did!' said Copic. 'What was it?'

'A monster sent to kill us all!' Muerta laughed, goggle eyed. 'A prehistoric beast risen from the Golya swamps!'

'It must be some kind of secret weapon we're testing,' said Tomsky. 'That or the first of the Germans.'

'No,' said Kasper, 'it's an omen, an omen from the gods. It means we're all going to live.'


For Mishka Babel the evening had been another disillusioning experience. He had joined the NKVD with high expectations, almost all of which had failed to be realised. Far from entering an elite dedicated to protecting the existence of the young Soviet state, Babel had found a lowly and cunning organisation dedicated to its own expansion. His colleagues, so unlike the students he had once mixed with at the Karl Marx University in Leipzig, were a mixture of whoremasters, imbeciles and cynical life-haters, furious at the idealism that they had discarded. Tonight had been by far the worst example of declining standards he had thus witnessed, an experience even more distasteful than having to stand in on an interrogation, a duty that was at least necessary if not altogether savoury. There was no doubt about it, though, the whole organisation was moving in a very unwholesome direction, and it would take nothing less than a bottom-up purge to improve matters. Babel smiled at the thought. A shaken-up NKVD would be a very different proposition to the current circus, one in which a committed communist like himself might finally make some progress.

Taking the short cut to his lodgings, Babel crossed Red Square and stopped underneath the giant Red Flag that was fluttering above the Lenin Mausoleum. It was a truly wonderful sight, the flag blowing first one way and then the other, like a giant torch pointing the way to the dispossessed of the world, telling them that one day the long night of capitalism would finish and that their day would come.

'It's beautiful, isn't it?'

Babel jumped back with fright; he had not realised that he was being watched.

'Where did you come from?' he asked shakily.

'From blood and piss and shit,' replied Makhno, stepping out of the shadows, 'and from what I read in *Pravda* I'm not the only one.'

'What are you doing here?'

'Experiencing the lightness and joy of being a communist. Just like you.'

'You've been drinking.'

'I most certainly have.' Makhno laughed. 'Come on; walk with me for a while. We can talk about Marx and Engels, God and angels, the good times and the bad . . .'

Nervously Babel accepted Makhno's offer, and together the two men set off into the early morning darkness.

# Chapter Nine

---

*Thursday*

Hubbard surveyed the desolate aerodrome with studied distaste; even by Soviet standards it was a truly awful sight to wake up to. The dawn mist had cleared to reveal a near-deserted landing strip being cleared by an old woman with a broom. Near her, a single two-door aeroplane was being readied for take-off. Hubbard looked over at the woman again. Her expression showed no interest in either him or her work.

'How Russian of her,' he heard himself say aloud. 'I suppose if anything crashes in this place, she's brought out to sweep it off the tarmac, and after a few months the bereaved are sent a telegram, complete with a spiffing great Red Star on the letter heading, of course.'

'You keep your filthy trap shut, Hubbard. We don't need to take any more of your pontificating faggotry. You're lucky as it is. If it was down to me you'd be leaving here in a coffin and not a plane.'

'Oh, really, Klimt, there's no need to come on like that. Ever since you chucked me into that truck this morning, all you boys have done is shout, shout, shout . . .'

'Move,' said Grotsky, poking his revolver into Hubbard's back. 'No more talking, just move.'

Hubbard flinched, sure now that the worst was really happening to him; they really were sending him back to London.

To his left Cretor stood watching, his contorted face darkening under a malevolent smile. 'Bye-bye, pretty boy, say hello to all the guards at Buckingham Palace for me . . .' he minced, waving his hand exaggeratedly and blowing a kiss.

'It'll be good for all of us to see the back of you, Hubbard,' Grotsky added, his hungover features shifting between dark blue and pale grey. 'The fairies over at Intelligence might have rated you, but for me and the rest of us you were always just trouble.'

'Now hold on there, Grotsky, hold on for just one minute. You don't really intend to put me on that flying machine over there, do you?'

'Do I detect a sudden hint of panic in your voice?' Grotsky laughed, the sadist in him starting to warm to his task.

'But I thought I was just being brought out here to be taught a lesson, I mean, given a fright, you know, to be shown what would happen to me if I didn't behave in future. Tell me I'm not wrong, please?'

'Well, my word, we really have pampered your dick-loving arse, haven't we? An ordinary Soviet citizen would have been happy to still have his life at this point, with ten years' worth of hard labour to look forward to, but here you are, in similar circumstances, flapping your arms around like a great big duck in a dress. I'm surprised you haven't asked me for a lawyer! Do you hear that, Cretor, I'm surprised he hasn't asked me for a lawyer!'

Hubbard could feel his jaw start to rattle and his palms moisten. Life without Russia was a life not worth living, even if it did mean sharing the same continent as the Grotskys of this world. He had not even minded them too much, especially since before this morning they had always been kept in check by some sympathetic higher power. Curiously, and quite erroneously, he had always assumed that they may have felt the same way about him, and if they did not actually like him, then they certainly might hold some rough type of affection for him.

'Would you like a lawyer?' Grotsky sneered menacingly. 'Because if you do we could always arrange to find you one of our Soviet lawyers. Isn't that right, Cretor? Yes, we could get one of our Soviet prosecutors that you write so favourably of, for your London papers. That way you'd know that you were in safe hands. Good, safe socialist hands.'

Hubbard held his finger to his nose. Not only did Grotsky's breath smell worse than a funeral for the undead, but his coat stank like the Great Fire of London. Something about his, and Cretor's, demeanour suggested that the previous forty-eight hours had been unusually hard on them, and it was up to Hubbard to act as the windbreak for their shared misfortune.

'But Grotsky, you simply can't do this to me. I mean, I was *happy* here, happy for the first time in my whole life, for God's sake.'

'*Happy?*' Grotsky almost choked on the word. 'By God, Hubbard, you've really made me angry now. Happy!' he exclaimed again. 'Have you any idea what we real communists think of your happiness? Do you want to know how stupid your happiness looks to us?'

'Steady on, Grotsky, ours is a mutually complementary relationship, after all, even if you think that I am an awful cad who uses your country like a bordello . . .'

'I couldn't have put it better myself . . .'

'You must still realise that my propaganda value for you has been enormous.'

'Which is exactly why we'll ask for a replacement, though this time we'll make sure he's vetted first. It's about time you realised that we've got better things to do than act like one of your British nannies, bailing you out every time you humiliate yourself . . .'

'But when did I last do that?'

'This morning, when you were found goat drunk in Gorky Park dressed up like a woman begging tramps for blowjobs. And in orange boots, for the love of God!'

'But I've already tried to explain that I was locked out of my apartment . . .'

'Bollocks. You weren't in a fit enough condition to even be washed . . .'

'I'd like to know how your spies worked that one out, Grotsky. I know they watch things, of course they watch things, but they don't notice very much, at least nothing that's very important. Nothing like what I've been able to procure for you over these past two years.'

'Hubbard, get on that plane before I shoot you right here.'

Doing as he was told, Hubbard walked up to the little stepladder leaning against the side of the plane. He wanted to ask whether his baggage would be sent after him but decided, given the circumstances, that this was unlikely to elicit a friendly response.

'I just want to say, before I get on the steps and it's too late, that whatever you think of me, and whatever I might think of you, coming to your country has been an incredible learning experience for me, and it's a fantastic thing that you people have achieved here, and I mean that with all my heart. In fact, I'd consider it an honour to shake your hand.'

Grotsky nearly bent double with laughter. 'You ought to know better than to shake hands with a secret policeman. Get on that plane and don't come back, because if you do you'll be sent down to hell in such a state that even "Old Nick" would be sick at the sight of you. Go on, fuck off.'

Hubbard turned and climbed up the steps. As he got to the top he stopped briefly to take one last look at the great white vastness of the Russian sky and, without realising it, he cried tears, lonely English tears, far, far from home.

Tomsky entered the office and picked up the broken lock. Gently he kicked the couch Copic was sprawled over and cleared his throat. Copic, like a dinosaur disturbed in hibernation, opened a cautious eye and asked, 'Where the fuck am I?'

'In our office. You've started to use it like a cave.'

Slowly Copic pulled himself up into a sitting position, tugging his shoulders back so as to stop the hangover from pushing him down again. There was something wrong with him, something more than just a hangover. Carefully he ran his hand down his chest and stopped. His hand felt damp and sticky. He looked down.

'Jesus Christ, Tomsky! Please tell me that this blood isn't my own!'

'It's radish sauce from the pudding you fell asleep on last night.'

'By God, thank you for that!'

'Would you like to be filled in on your movements, or at least those that I know of, over the past twelve hours?'

'No, not unless I made a complete cunt of myself in front of the players.'

'You didn't do that. But you were very worried about something that I think we should speak about right away.'

'Good, then,' said Copic, deliberately ignoring Tomsky's inference. 'All's well that ends well ... Christ, what about those shooting stars! I didn't imagine them, did I?'

'No, we all saw it.'

'Well then, we've got to tell someone about it! It

was . . . I've never seen so many of them in one place in my life!'

'And who are we going to tell?'

'*Pravda*?'

'They already know.' Tomsky dropped the paper on the desk. 'There, at the bottom of the front page. Read it.'

Copic studied the paper distrustfully. 'This . . . this is bollocks. They say here that our radar picked up on a squadron, a squadron I tell you, of Finnish or Polish spotter planes, but didn't shoot them down . . . because they didn't want to provoke war!'

'I know, I read the piece to the rest of the boys this morning.'

'"This is another provocation for war that our leaders wish to avoid, for fear of losing Soviet lives." What bollocks! What we saw last night weren't spotter planes, they were shooting stars . . .'

'Perhaps you'd like to tell that to the editor of *Pravda* . . .'

'But others must have seen what we did. We can't have been the only ones. They can't fob us all off like that.'

'Can't they? Don't they do it all the time? I agree with you, of course they weren't spotter planes. And I'd be surprised if *Pravda* thinks they are, or even if our military do, but that's not the point. They don't like mysteries or imponderable situations, they like to give things a name and then pretend that without the name the thing can't exist . . . as far as I know there aren't any "Soviet experts" on shooting stars, but several on planes, which pretty much settles the question as far as our press is concerned.'

'So . . .'

'You're missing my point,' said Tomsky impatiently. 'In a perfect life of course I'd like the two of us to climb to the top of Spassky Tower every night with a telescope and see whether we can spot any more of those things, but that's not going to happen . . .'

'Hold on . . .'

'. . . because unless we choose right this Saturday not one of us is ever going to play the violin again. You can talk about astronomy until you reach old age but we've more pressing problems at hand . . .'

'I know, I know. For God's sake, I've just woken up, man . . .'

'Turn to the back page of that *Pravda* . . .'

'Why?'

'Just do it.'

Copic turned the paper over and a look of horror spread over his face.

'There's an interview with me here, an interview I never gave . . .'

'I know. Let me save you some time. The upshot of this delightful piece, no doubt put in by our friends over at Dynamo, is that you, our illustrious manager, admit that our winning run may have come to an end . . .'

'I what?'

'Come to an end because of the enormous technical

progress made by our rivals Dynamo, under the steely leadership of the great Klimt Grotsky.'

'What the hell is that meant to mean . . .'

'Mean to whom? To the public it's an admission of fallibility that'll break them in gently for when we lose on Saturday. For us it is a warning to lose on Saturday, and for the hack that put the piece together just a job. We no more fit into their world than the shooting stars over Radek's house. They don't know what to make of us, or how to use us, so instead they'll have to be content to destroy us. If not on Saturday then soon, win, lose or draw.'

Copic scratched his chin and gazed ruefully out of the window. 'Here, help me out of these, I look like some kind of fucking disaster. In fact, get Muerta in with my old tracksuit. This one's losing its shine.'

The office door tilted slightly and Josip's head peered around it cautiously. 'I hope I'm not interrupting anything, but the door's off its hinges and I'm afraid I'd have broken it completely if I had knocked.'

'Knock the thing off and wear it for a hat for all I care . . .'

'Consider us at your service.' Tomsky grinned. 'The boss and I were just discussing something that concerns all of you.'

Josip walked in, his posture crouched and tentative. Behind him followed Makhno and Kasper.

'Good things come in threes, eh?' groaned Copic. 'And what bad tidings can I expect from you lot today? The forcible takeover of our club by those things I saw flying over Radek's last night or just the news that Grotsky's agreed to let me take over at Dynamo for him?'

Makhno smiled gingerly. 'No, none of the above. Not today anyway.'

'Then what, pray?'

'We all know about what happened to you and Tomsky at the meeting on Tuesday. And we all know what we think of it.'

'I won't say I'm surprised to hear that the gossip has already done its rounds . . .'

'We wanted to say that we all support you in the position you and Tomsky have taken. That we, the senior players, and the rest of the boys are right behind you all the way.'

'Our position?' said Tomsky. 'I wasn't aware that we had a position, or that if we did you knew what it was . . .'

'You don't have to lie to us to protect us, we all know the score. If the "comrades" haven't got us one way then they've got us another. At least this way we all go out fighting.'

'Excellent, Makhno!' said Copic, thumping the table. 'Just the talk I like to hear coming from my team captain!'

'Are you sure you've discussed this with everyone?' asked Tomsky. 'This isn't the kind of decision you can come to lightly, and there are a lot of people around the team that this will affect too . . .'

'What's there to discuss?' said Copic. 'You've heard

what the boys have to say, they've all spoken with one voice, so what's the point in any more of those unnecessary discussions you love so much? We've been given our veto, and it says action!'

'God almightly.' Tomsky sighed. 'You're still drunk, aren't you? All you need is a little encouragement and any doubts you have fly straight out of the window.'

'Excuse me, Comrades,' came a voice from the door. 'Would you all please accept my most humble and sincere apologies.'

'Radek!' exclaimed Tomsky with surprise. 'What the fuck are you doing here?'

Ignoring the new face in the room, Copic said, 'Sometimes I wonder what the matter is with you, Tomsky. Here we are, supposedly living in an age of collectivism, and yet everywhere I look it's every man for himself. Yet here we have some of our boys sticking their necks out and falling in behind us, and the first thing you do is try and change their minds!'

'Easy, boss, I think the game's moved on again,' said Tomsky, leading a nervous Radek in by the arm.

'Mother of Kazan! What's he doing here? Doesn't anyone warn me about anything?'

'Believe me, boss, this is the first we knew of it.' Makhno grinned cheekily. 'Though I'm not sure why it should be so shocking to see a centre-forward in his manager's office.'

'Don't come the leery yak with me, Makhno, you know exactly why my teeth are standing on end. Satan's beard, my boy, what are you doing here?'

Radek, taken aback and embarrassed, bent his head down and spoke into his hand. 'I want to play again.'

'Speak up, lad, I can hardly hear you.'

'I want to play again, boss. For myself, for you, but most of all for the fans and for the team.'

'What the hell . . . Why, my prayers are answered. The stars, you're right, Kasper, they were an omen, an omen that our boy's come back to us!'

'This is quite a change of heart, Radek. May I ask what prompted it?'

'Of course, Comrade Tomsky, it was guilt and shame – guilt at wasting my own talent and shame at letting everyone else down. I can see how selfish I was, thinking only of my own pain all the time.'

'Well, I'm delighted to hear it!'

'Tell me something, kid,' said Makhno, 'does this decision have anything to do with your woman? Has she come back to you or did you decide to do this off your own back?'

'No, no, that hasn't happened. This has nothing to do with Katya.'

'Then what has happened? Because when I saw you last night you didn't look like you were ready to change your mind. In fact, we didn't even mention the subject of football directly.'

'A dream, Makhno. In my drunken sleep I dreamed that I'd have to make this decision.'

'Stop bothering the boy! Who bloody cares why he's back, the important thing is that he is back!'

Makhno laughed sceptically. 'Oh, I'm happy all

right, Igor Ivanovich, his young legs are going to save my old ones a lot of work, but I'd still like to hear about this dream. Even you'd have to admit that it's not every day that we take our instructions in our sleep.'

'There's nothing much to it, Nestor, nothing much that I can remember anyway, only that I was wandering around the corridors of this beautiful Byzantine castle listening to some wonderful singing . . .'

'Was it Katya's voice you could hear?' Makhno winked at Tomsky. 'Or perhaps some fallen Turkish angels?'

'I don't know, but the music was so lovely that I found it hard to stay on my feet. Listening to it was like becoming drunk and I kept staggering into these shapes, ghosts perhaps . . .'

'What were they doing there?'

'Speaking to me in holy voices, saying that I will have to live with or without her, but that I must live to play football and move the masses . . . because without that I'm no different to any other boy with a broken heart.'

'By Christ!' Copic sighed. 'Now I really have heard it all, Kasper. I leave this madman in your highly incapable charge! Clearly the days of worrying whether a forward's play is pretty fucking scratchy or not are over – nowadays it's all angelic visions and love songs! Wait until Grotsky hears of this. I'll be damned if he'll have the courage to lace his bootstraps without getting a priest's blessing first!'

'This is brilliant news, Radek. I'm glad your dreams

are cheering you up for a change, but there is something else we need to settle first . . .'

'Oh, for God's sake, Tomsky, don't ruin the moment. Radek's gone from feeling like a boy to thinking like a man . . .'

There was a cough from the far corner of the room and Muerta edged open the half-broken door.

'Come in, come in, the more the merrier, my girl! Pull yourself up a pew, we were about to conduct a seance.'

Muerta coughed again, her throat tight with fear, and pointed to the telephone on the desk. 'Copic, you had better pick up the phone. There's a call for you and I think you need to deal with it right away.'

'You know I never take calls when I'm on duty. Now don't mind these others, I feel comfortable in the presence of madness – take the call in the next room and then come in and join us for some vodka. Radek's back – bless my arse he is!'

'You'll take this call. It's Stalin.'

It was a long second before Copic picked up the receiver.

'This is Igor Ivanovich Copic . . . hello?'

'Hello, Igor Ivanovich, this is Josef Vissarionovich. How are you?'

'I'm . . . very well. A little tired but very well.'

'Good, good.'

'How are you?'

'The same, you know how it is, always work. That's why men of your calibre are of such use to us, Copic; you make us forget about work.'

'Honoured to be of service . . .' Copic felt his tongue turn cold. 'I mean, how can I be of service to you, Josef Vissarionovich?'

'Ha! Of course, when men like us talk there is always a reason.' Stalin cleared his throat. Copic heard him put the phone to one side, and sip from a glass of water. Copic imagined he could feel the water sinking deep into Stalin's stomach.

'Are you still there Copic?'

'Yes, yes I am Josef Vissarionovich.'

'The people have been working too hard of late. We have given them too much to do and too little time to do it, you agree?'

'Yes . . .'

'They need a holiday, we all do. The match will be brought forward by a day. You will play tomorrow. The people will have an extra day to relax and so will your players, now that they can miss a day of training. This way we will all be happy. Could you do this for me, Copic?'

'Of course, Josef Vissarionovich, the sooner the better, that's what I say!'

'Good man, good man. Keep up the good work and give the people a show, Copic, we both know they need one.'

'Don't worry about that, we will all right, and thank you, Josef Vissarionovich, thank you!'

The line went dead.

'Jesus bloody Christ! That was the fucking *Boss*, fucking Stalin!' spluttered Copic.

'What did he say?' said Tomsky, grabbing Copic's arm. 'What did he fucking say?'

'What's he like?' shouted Muerta. 'What's he like?'

'Jesus Christ, can you believe it, that was Stalin!' said Tomsky to Makhno.

'I know, Tomsky, I fucking know! Come on, Copic, don't just sit there like that, tell us what he said!'

'No, tell us what he's like!' repeated Muerta.

'What's he like, eh?' mused Copic, pouring a cup of cold tea over his head. 'I'd say . . . I'd say that he's a bit on the shy side.'

Muerta looked at Tomsky and they both started laughing.

'Game on,' said Copic, ignoring them, 'game on!'

Radek walked out of the Spartak building and down the snow-covered steps to the bus stop. He felt good about life; good about his friends and good about the way he would lead the team out with Makhno the following day. He felt all of this because, deep in his heart, he hoped Katya would be watching.

'Hello, Radek,' a friendly passer-by called. 'Good to see you back, boy!'

'It's good to be back!' Radek smiled, and then turned red. It seemed like such a silly thing to say. A sledge rattled by and Radek rubbed a little snow on his cheeks to control the blushing. Not noticing Radek's discomfort, the secret policeman walked on, happy to have elicited a response from a Spartak player at last.

'I'm ready to put a few roubles on that being another

one of their snoopers – he looks just like the bastard who follows me in to training every morning,' said Makhno, leaning against the iron lantern next to the potato kiosk.

'No, he looks too carefree to be one of the comrades. Look, he's even got a spring in his step,' replied Tomsky.

'That could mean that he's secured a conviction.'

Tomsky kicked at a frozen clot of gravel. 'So what do you make of the phone call from our great leader?'

Makhno scratched his nose cautiously, a little embarrassed at having been as excited as everyone else when Stalin had rung. 'It could mean anything, couldn't it? Everyone knows that the Boss likes playing games . . .'

'Copic seems to have taken it at face value . . .'

'That's because he wants to . . .' Makhno said, shaking his head.

'But he said there was something in Stalin's voice that he trusted, or that at least, made him believe that he was being sincere. And Copic *was* the one who talked to him . . .'

'*Trusted! Sincere!* You should hear yourself, Tomsky! This is Stalin we're talking about, not one of Kasper's religious icons. Think of the number of men who thought they enjoyed Stalin's confidences and remember where they are now.'

'I know that, but the point is that he asked Copic to make a game of it.'

'Wrong. He told Copic that he had "to give the people a show". Now you could interpret that in a number of ways, which is why the sadistic bastard takes such pleasure in giving us these scraps to chew on . . . Come on, let's walk.'

'"Give the people a show."' Tomsky frowned. 'No, I can see what you mean. Giving them a show could mean making a convincing job of losing the game on purpose . . . is that what you think?'

'Or it might just mean giving them a show. It depends on how optimistic you're feeling.'

'And how optimistic are you feeling?' Tomsky asked, trying to look as unconspiratorial as possible.

'I don't know. There are no rational grounds for optimism – you only have to live with your eyes open to see that . . . and like you I think they'll come for us sooner or later, though like Copic I think playing up to being buffoons has been our best defence so far . . .'

'I'm not sure how much of it is "playing up" . . .'

'Then we're in exactly the same position we were in before this phone call was made; we can play their game and join them in the secret. But then we become insiders and, as we all know, insiders conspire to sign their own death warrants . . .'

'Like the public trials. Yes, I've noticed that the Party is getting keener on blaming its own people for its mistakes.'

'They have to,' said Makhno. 'Its own kind know all about its compromises and imperfections and all the other sleights of hand required for the success of "Socialism in One Country". Choosing to play Grotsky's game may not be the passage to freedom it first appears. It could just be the beginning of the end, since if his star falls we'll follow. But if we look at it that way either of our choices is as dangerous as the other. At least as outsiders we've been considered too lowly to warrant the leadership's attention. That may change as of Saturday, but if I have to die, let it be for something I'll actually do, and, if you'll pardon my naivety, really believe in.'

'Aren't you dramatising the situation?' Tomsky asked nervously. 'If they do anything to us, and you've admitted that they may not, since for all we know we're just pawns in a struggle between Grotsky and Stalin, it'd be a stretch in the camps, and not death . . .'

Makhno spread out his palms as if they were weights measuring two different fates. 'Quite a difference, but I dare say you're right. So now we've outlined the hugely regrettable table of choices at our disposal, which do we prefer?'

'I guess we forget about the rest and play football.'

'There isn't a man in the team that'll disagree with that.'

'Are you sure? You know, they may be a team but that doesn't mean that they'll all act like a single person . . .'

'After all we've been through I have trouble thinking of one that won't.'

Tomsky rubbed his eyes. 'Well, I can think of at least one . . .'

'Koba?'

'Who else would I mean . . .'

'He may be an informer but that won't make any difference to the way he plays. Even Grotsky can understand that. He simply hasn't the complexity to pretend to be anything other than what he is when out on the pitch. It's the same with any of them that want to bottle it. How can they? We win, or lose, as a team.'

'I hope you're right about that. That wasn't what was concerning me so much, though perhaps it should've. What I can't understand is why they chose Koba. And how have they managed to keep the big lummox so tight lipped about it?'

'His thick-headedness might have been a factor but I reckon it's also got something to do with his old man. He used to be a kulak and run a medium-size estate, but from what I hear he got into bed with the Party. They even made him manager of his local collective farm. Perhaps they told Koba that something that wasn't so nice might happen to the old boy, and his six daughters, if he didn't play ball with them. With simple men like Koba the best way of reaching them is usually through someone else . . . it would probably have been much simpler for them if they had tried to tap you or me,' Makhno added with a laugh.

'That figures, as Koba doesn't strike me as the kind to fear for his own life. I know there's nothing we can do for him at the moment, and that it's probably too late to do anything now, but I think we should sound him out in some way and ask . . .'

'Are you mad, Tomsky? And then do what? Ask him

to become a double agent on our behalf? You must be crazy. Let's keep it simple. Come Monday morning, if any of us are still here, we arrange for him to have a nasty leg injury as the result of an ill-timed tackle. That way he's free of his dilemma, and we're free of a spy.'

Tomsky brushed a layer of snow off his sleeve. 'Let's hope it's as simple as that.'

Makhno shrugged his shoulders nonchalantly. 'We can only worry about the things that are in our power to fix.'

'What's that supposed to mean?'

Makhno raised an eyebrow and shrugged again.

'Right, let's make sure that every member of tomorrow's starting line-up, apart from Radek, who could probably use the sleep, knows what the score is. I don't want anyone there because he feels he has to be.'

Makhno picked up his kitbag and followed Tomsky down the street to the players' lounge, the midday sun rolling down the bridge of his nose like a reminder of all he could lose.

Two miles away at the Dynamo training ground Augustus Koba reviewed his options. In five minutes Grotsky and Cretor would arrive and ask him what he had got for them. It was no good fending them off with more harmless anecdotes or inconsequential gossip; he had done that too many times before and they were wise to it now. All that was left for him to do was betray his friends, report the seditious conversations, polemics against Stalin, and non-Party opinions he had been privy to for these past four years, and consider himself lucky that he was the informer, and not the one informed on. That would mean the end of the team he loved and played for but would, at least, guarantee the continuity of his own life.

Koba looked out of the window at the Dynamo players doing push-ups in the snow, thought of his sisters in Irkutsk, took the revolver out of his pocket and blew his head off.

His death was not reported until Saturday, a day after the match. His team mates all played in the belief that he had let them down by staying away.

# Chapter Ten

By the time Slovo reached Gorky Park it was already turning dark, the moon emerging like a white eye from the patches of cloud hanging in the coal-grey sky. Ignoring a sign that read 'THE GRASS IS THE PEOPLE'S – KEEP OFF IT!', Slovo skipped over the chain wall and cut across a patch of freezing weeds towards the main bandstand. To his right a large bronze bear looked on indifferently, sandwiched between a cluster of dying elm and beech trees planted forty years earlier by the American ambassador. Moving nimbly, to avoid the groups of children skating down the frozen paths, he crossed the mock Japanese bridge, erected a month before the Russo-Japanese War of 1905, and took his place on a bench overlooking the open-air theatre. Sitting beside him was Lotya Pantya. Below them a troop of heavily wrapped up ballerinas, looking like white tennis balls, were practising a special outdoor version of *Swan Lake* to be held in honour of a famous Irish playwright who had decided, along with a famous English poet, that the Soviet Union was a workers' paradise, and had travelled to Moscow to attest to the fact.

'Do you like the ballet?' asked Lotya.

'I don't know much about it. I prefer Slav dances; they're a good way of releasing energy. That's what Copic says anyway.'

Lotya looked at Slovo carefully, hoping that she had not made a mistake in her appraisal of his character. 'You're a Russian, Slovo, so you must have a natural appreciation of ballet; it's part of your birthright. Vitality and discipline, they're the secret of ballet and of gymnastics – and football too, I should say.'

Slovo nodded politely. As far as he knew there was no secret to football; one just played it, and sometimes enjoyed it very much, and that was all.

'Come on,' said Lotya, taking Slovo's hand, 'let's go somewhere more private. It's possible we could be watched here. Grotsky has spies, or people who want to be his spies, in every corner of this city. I don't feel comfortable anywhere.'

Carefully, the two proceeded in single file down the slope to an abandoned old monastery, now doubling as a storage depot, perched by a loop in the frozen river. A few yellow and green tiles hung from its side, but most had been knocked off by the wind and years of decay. Its crumbling red-brick base now stood only a few feet from the advancing river bank.

'I wish they would look after these old buildings,' said Lotya. 'I think they're beautiful in their own way.'

Slovo smiled. Lotya had a slightly pompous way of talking that he hadn't noticed before. 'One day someone might say the same thing about those statues of Stalin, up there by the gates, when people who aren't even born yet let the birds shit on them.'

Lotya glanced at Slovo's enormous grinning face and giggled. 'I hope you're right. I hate them.' She was about to add that she knew she shouldn't say things like this, as she did not know Slovo well enough yet, but gazing at his adoring face made her realise that this was unnecessary and that they had wasted enough time.

'You've thought about what we've talked about, haven't you?'

'Of course I have,' said Slovo, who had, since Tomsky's briefing on the dilemma of Saturday's match, been forced to think about a lot of things.

'And you still want to go through with it?'

'Why wouldn't I? I'd do anything for us to be together.'

'But you know it won't be easy – having to kill a man, I mean.'

'It will be if it's Grotsky. Just tell me when.'

'One night next week. I don't know which yet, but on whichever one he first goes out to get drunk.'

'I'll be on call when you need me.'

'And you can forget the business with the axe we talked about before – it isn't necessary. All we need to do is stuff a cloth in his mouth when he's asleep and sit on him. It'll look like an accident then. And afterwards, once he's dead and everything's cleared up, you'll be able to look after me.' She smiled and touched his face. 'You know, I'd probably have killed him before but I needed to know that there was someone else who would look after me after he was gone, and now that I've found you I don't need to worry any more.' Lotya smiled again, pleased at the way the honest and the Machiavellian sat side by side in her character, without troubling the essential purity of her conscience or enterprise.

Slovo lifted his head up and beamed proudly. 'And what about leaving the country? When are we going to do that?'

'I thought about that last night and decided that it might be a little unrealistic for now. I mean, they don't let just anyone leave the country and we don't want to break the law. I think we should be sensible for now and just take it one step at a time.'

Slovo looked a little disappointed but, not wishing to be disagreeable, said, 'I guess you're right to say that we should be careful at first, and it's obvious that you're much better at making plans than me, but I still think we should go abroad some time. I was thinking of Paris. Apparently they play football there too and all the French workers, peasants and journalists love us Russians . . .'

Lotya's mind was already elsewhere as she glanced over her shoulder and said, 'Right, help me break down this door. I know it's rotten but it's still too heavy for me to do it on my own.'

Slovo started. 'Why?'

'So we can go inside and make love, silly.'

Slovo did not need to be asked twice. With the same

passion he would discover in the midst of the sexual act, the diminutive centre-half took a running jump at the door and broke it down in one go. Behind him Lotya clapped her hero on, the snowflakes falling like feathers on the hood of her red coat.

The secret policeman wiped the snow off his field glasses and wondered what to do next. He smiled; no one had asked him to tail Lotya and Slovo, it had been his own brainchild, but it was a dangerous one. It was precisely because he had suspected something like this that he hadn't told Grotsky of his intention to follow his mistress. But what was he to do now that he had? Grotsky hadn't asked him to snoop on Lotya, and though he might be grateful for this zealous devotion to duty, there was no way to be certain of what his response would be. The secret policeman scratched his head; in a situation like this it was hard enough to guess what any ordinary man would do, let alone a borderline schizophrenic like Grotsky. No one enjoyed discovering that he was a cuckold, and regardless of what the final outcome would be, there was always a strong chance that the messenger would end up getting shot. The secret policeman spat into the snow, slung the field glasses over his shoulder and scuttled down the bank, certain that he was alive in an age in which initiative would not find its rewards this side of the grave.

'Don't draw the curtains, I like to leave them open.'

'So do I, I just thought that you might not,' said Muerta.

'No, I enjoy the light and the view,' said Tomsky.

'Me too!'

Tomsky bent his head a little to one side, as if to give Muerta the chance to admit that she was being sarcastic.

'No! I really do! I love the way the street lamp makes the room glow,' she said, blowing out a candle and taking her place next to Tomsky on the couch. 'It makes me feel warm and secure. I could spend Christmas in this place!'

Tomsky held Muerta's face up to his own and kissed her, noticing that she shut her eyes as he did so. Pulling away slightly, but not so much as to destroy their tentatively established bond, he said, 'You talk a lot about feeling secure in places. Is that because you don't . . .' He paused and tried to change his probing tone. 'I don't mean that you aren't secure now, but before this, during your life in Spain. Do you find it difficult to trust people because of what happened to you there?'

Muerta looked at him as if this was the first time she had ever had to think before answering a question. 'How do you mean?'

'In the way that some people are never secure anywhere. With your old boyfriends, for instance, back in Spain, but not just there with them, but anywhere with anyone.'

Muerta turned her nose up and pulled at an earlobe.

It was the closest thing Tomsky had seen in her to an affectation. 'I think to trust someone is to be bored by them,' she said haughtily.

'No it isn't, it's to love them,' said Tomsky, careful to prevent himself from adding that he thought her aloofness was akin to insecurity, as he was sure he was sounding patronising enough already.

Muerta looked down at him for a moment and he noticed her thick lips quiver. Without saying anything she pulled off her shawl and fell on him like a dead weight. She was crying and he could feel her warm tears on his face.

'Why do you ask me whether I feel secure here when I know perfectly well that you intend to get us all killed over your stupid game . . .'

'I never told you that would happen. It won't.'

'No, but I could tell from the look on your face when you came in tonight.'

'Listen, I have enough to bloody worry about without you making heavy weather . . .'

There was a knock on the door. Muerta sprang up at once, arranged her hair and withdrew to the adjoining bedroom. 'You had better get that – it could be important.'

Tomsky got up unwillingly, not sure whether this was what she actually wanted him to do, or whether she wanted him to tell whoever was on the other side of the door to go to hell.

After opening it, and realising it was Radek, he wished he had.

'Hello, Comrade Tomsky. If I'm disturbing you I'll leave right away.'

'Leave? I haven't even let you in yet . . .'

'Is that you Radek?' called Muerta. 'Come in. I was just about to make some tea, then I'll come in and join you both . . . that is unless there's something you both need to discuss privately.'

Radek peered over Tomsky's shoulder bashfully. 'I'm sorry, Muerta, but, um, there is . . . a private matter I need Tomsky's advice about.'

'Not to worry.' Muerta smiled. 'I'll be in the bedroom. You boys give me a knock when you've finished.'

Grudgingly Tomsky stepped out of Radek's way and let him in.

'I'm sorry if I've interrupted anything.'

'No, not at all, I usually sit in the dark with a woman when I have nothing better to do.'

Radek paused. 'Hmm, yes. Me and Katya used to do that too. I took it as a sign of how comfortable and happy we were in each other's company.'

Tomsky raised an eyebrow. 'There isn't some new problem between you and Katya that you've come here to tell me about? . . . something that's going to stop you from playing tomorrow . . .'

'No, no, don't worry, it's nothing like that. Not a new problem anyway.'

'What? So you mean you *have* changed your mind about playing?'

'No! I'll still play tomorrow.'

'Then what is it?'

'It's about something that happened, that Katya used to do, I mean, when we were together, that I never really thought about at the time. But when I think about it now it sort of bothers me. This has been happening a lot, actually. I end up thinking back to some problem we had, and then I have trouble getting out of the thought, if you see what I mean. And then that makes me feel bad about everything else.'

Tomsky shook his head and slumped down on the couch. 'There're some matches on the table and a candle over there. Light it; I feel like it's going to be a long night.'

'Thanks, Tomsky!' Radek laughed. 'The others are always trying to prise the details out of me, but I feel like you're the only one who really listens and understands!'

'No, thank you, Radek, rest assured that I'm hon-oured to be your confidant.'

Radek nodded gratefully. 'It's funny how difficult it is to talk to people about our problems . . .'

'So get on and tell me about them,' interrupted Tomsky.

'This is a very personal thing I'm about to describe . . .'

'Radek . . .'

'All right. Well, Katya, when we . . . when we were about to . . . to mate together.'

'*Mate!*' Tomsky nearly choked.

'Be intimate with each other, if you see what I mean.'

'Of course I see what you mean, you bloody fool!'

Radek blushed and lowered his head. 'I knew it was stupid trying to bring this up in front of someone else . . .'

'Far from it, Radek! You're a bottomless pit of interest. Please continue!'

'If you're sure you want me to . . .'

Tomsky nodded impatiently.

'Right, I'll just have to get this out in one go. What would happen is that she wouldn't let me touch her thing with my hand.'

'You mean she didn't allow you to have sex with her?'

'No, no, we had that all the time, and loved it very much, that's not what I'm saying.'

'Then help me, Radek, be more specific.'

'If you don't mind me being crude, she wouldn't let me touch her vagina with my hand or fingers.'

'So . . .'

'So what she would do was guide my cock in with her hand. She'd never let me do it, and never let me touch her down there first.'

'But she was always wet when she took your cock in her?'

'Yes. Most of the time anyway.'

Resisting the urge to laugh helplessly, Tomsky asked, 'So what exactly is the problem here, other than her not being around to have sex with you any more?'

'The business of the hand, of course!' said Radek, the exasperation showing on his face. 'I can't help but feel that if I could just solve that riddle, everything else would become clear to me, and I'd understand why she isn't here now.'

Tomsky sat up in his chair and looked Radek straight in the face. Radek stared back unfazed, his eyes unblinking.

Tomsky whistled slowly, playing for time. Radek was completely mad, of that there was no doubt, so reasoning with him was hopeless. That left only one other option; he would have to humour him and play him at his own game.

'That certainly is a difficult one, Radek, but I agree with you, there must be an answer out there somewhere . . .'

'That's exactly what I think, Tomsky, that's why the whole thing's been troubling me so much.'

'Well, we've got to get to the bottom of it, then.'

'If you could . . .'

'Now let me see. You say that she let you enter her with your prick, but not actually touch her "there" with your hand, is that right?'

'Yes, that's it.'

'Well, think about it, what do you normally do with your hands?'

'What, all the time?'

'I mean what do you usually use your fingers and hands for?'

'Everything from cleaning my teeth to lacing my boots, I guess.'

'But what does any normal man use his prick for?'

'Taking a leak and . . . and having sex.'

'Just those two things? Are you sure a man only uses it for those two things?'

'Yes!' Radek almost protested.

'Exactly! There, can't you see it?'

Radek looked puzzled and shook his head.

'Look, having sex with you was obviously a very special thing for Katya, especially the part when you entered her. It was so precious that she'd only let those bits of you inside her that were meant to go in there and nowhere else. That's why she didn't let you use your hands. The only thing she believed your dick was for was for entering her. It was hers, and not something that should be used for anything else. Your hands, though, belonged to the world and to all the tasks they were built to do in it, which is why she didn't want them anywhere near her twat.'

Radek began to nod like a sage on the path to enlightenment.

'She must have felt the same way about her own genitals too. They were just as precious to her as yours were, that's why she didn't want them spoilt by things like your hands, which were brutalised and roughened by their daily contact with the world – in her opinion, I mean.'

Radek grabbed Tomsky's arm. 'So that's why she didn't want them down there . . . By God, Tomsky, you're right! You really *understand*, don't you? You've made the effort to see the world like she and I did, and understand it!'

'It's obvious from what you've told me that she

cared about you very deeply, and this whole business of the hands is further proof,' said Tomsky by way of conclusion.

Radek shook his head in amazement. 'It's crazy, you know, I spent most of this afternoon torturing myself over this, and all I could come up with was . . .'

'Was what?'

'Was that she must have thought I was a clumsy horse who couldn't be trusted to finger her sensitive parts.'

'Well, I'm glad I've helped you get rid of that illusion. Now that you're on your road to recovery the last thing you need to do is worry yourself with these little details . . . Oh, that reminds me. There was one thing that Katya said that took me by surprise. She said that it was your decision to end the relationship . . .'

'No, we took turns to do that all the time, every time we argued, in fact. It's just this time she actually left.'

Tomsky nodded in what might have been construed as sympathy. 'Well, that's all done with now . . .'

'You're right.' Radek smiled. 'And I thank you for your patience with me. I guess you know that I'm a bit sensitive in a way. Probably a bit more so than any of the other lads, I suppose.'

'To be honest I was fairly late in working that one out.'

'And me with you. Up until a few days ago I thought you were, well, a little cynical. That was what some of the boys said anyway.'

'Bless you, Radek, how wrong can you all be?'

'I know. I'm embarrassed about it now, believe me.'

'So you'll be turning out for us tomorrow, then,' said Tomsky, changing the subject.

'Of course.'

'Even though you still find yourself preoccupied with Katya . . .'

'I'll always be, Comrade, it's just something I'll have to get used to.'

'Good boy, Radek, that's the stuff,' said Tomsky, leading him to the door. 'And I don't suppose you've had time to practise your free kicks during your recent sabbatical?'

'You know, that's something I don't need to do,' said Radek confidently, a slight swagger in his step as he walked through the doorway, 'because I can see them all happen in here whenever I want to,' he added, tapping his head, 'before I've even taken them. That's why you and Copic make such a fuss over me, isn't it?'

'You know, Radek, you might yet make captain one day.' Tomsky winked as he closed the door.

'Do you think he will?' said Muerta, coming out of the bedroom.

'No.'

'Why not? Because he's immature?'

'No, because we'll all be dead before then,' said Tomsky flatly.

Muerta tried to smile in the dark, unsure of whose turn it was to cry now.

\*     \*     \*

Tomsky wasn't the only one occupied with thoughts of death that night. Lotya Pantya stood over Grotsky's sleeping body and tried to imagine him dead. Sadly, this was an easier thing to do than coming up with a way of actually killing him had been. She knew that she wanted to, there was no problem there, but her first plan, which had involved Slovo, a cupboard and an axe, had turned out to be a bad one. This was largely the fault of Slovo himself, who, despite initial appearances, was not the killer she had taken him to be. In fact, beneath his shaved head beat a soft brain and below that a simple heart. He was, she had decided, even complicated in a simple way. But this at least meant he could be trusted, or this was what she hoped, because what she was suggesting was enough to scare any sane man into the arms of the NKVD. Her second plan, involving suffocation with a cloth doused in bleach, was more practical, and therefore more plausible. The idea of the axe had probably just been a throwback to her life in the village, where anyone who was killed was always killed with an axe.

Lotya scowled; how had she ever got *used* to this life and the man who ran it without her consent? If she had only been able to recognise its abnormality earlier on she would never have found herself boxed into this corner, but that was her trouble; she was too adaptable. If she had been dropped into hell itself she would have found ways of surviving, and after survival she would have slipped into a daily routine.

Grotsky cursed and turned over on his side. Lotya sat down on the edge of the bed and took off her galoshes. She had, when things seemed hopeless, cheered herself up by thinking of her superior survival skills, and her ability to cope where others would give up and roll over. But the truth was less flattering; she was no more than a malleable puppet, shaped by, but incapable of shaping, life. Only her adventure with Slovo could change this because ... because it had to and she would kill herself if it did not. For Lotya there was no such thing as selfless love, it had no meaning. She loved Slovo, in as much as she thought of love at all, because he understood her and because of what he could do for her – wasn't all love like this?

Lotya could feel death again, not Grotsky's this time but her own. Closing her eyes, she began to pray. 'Don't fail me, Slovo, please don't fail me ...'

Cretor walked up to Babel and switched off his desk lamp. 'What are you still doing up here at this hour?'

'Working,' replied Babel with a shrug of his shoulders.

'Football stuff or police work?'

'Police reports. There's a huge backlog to be got through.'

'You don't really like the football side to this job, do you?'

'Why should I? There are more important things in life than that bloody game.'

Cretor looked at him for a moment before nodding slowly. 'I agree. Anyway, what's the quantity of football work compared to the police work, eh? Some people around here seem to have got things the wrong way round. Don't you think?'

Babel sat where he was and said nothing.

'Do you know something that puzzles me about you, Babel? Would you like me to tell you what it is?'

'You can do whatever you like, Comrade.'

'"You can do whatever you like, Comrade." Yes, I like that. What puzzles me about you is that I often get the distinct impression that you hate every person in this building and yet, when the chance comes to voice a complaint, not a word issues from your mouth. Now why is that? Why is it that you're the only person here who I don't hear badmouthing his colleagues behind their backs?'

'It's just not something I feel comfortable doing, Comrade Cretor,' said Babel cautiously.

'That may be so, but you'd be perfectly within your rights if you did when the time came, if you see what I mean – perfectly within your rights if the proper authority gave you the chance to say what you really think about certain colleagues who have, shall we say, failed to appreciate your talents, subtle as they are.'

Cretor grinned evilly and Babel attempted to return an equally diabolical grimace. 'Yes, I think I see what you mean now.'

'Of course you do. You're a clever kid, too clever to be buried under this paperwork every night whilst others we shan't speak of live the life of tsars. Yes, to never talk badly of someone suggests that you can't be someone who talks very much, but I get the feeling that once we start you talking about some of the things that go on around here it'll be difficult to get you to stop. Am I right?'

'For sure, Comrade.'

'Good. Now put those papers away and get on your way home. And be careful not to say anything to the chief about our little chat. He'd only jump to conclusions just like he always does.'

Babel nodded soberly and got to his feet, pleased to be on the march towards socialism at last.

The secret policeman, who had now failed to keep up with Copic's movements for the past eight hours, walked up to the booth, a small food parcel tucked under his arm. For once he did not resemble his usual self. On duty he was hard pressed to strike any kind of impression at all on passers-by. But tonight he stood out as only the sad and forlorn can.

The clerk in the booth looked him up and down sympathetically and shook his head. 'You can leave the food here but I've already told you that it'll do her no good. She's working on the canal now and there's no way it'll reach her. I'm sorry, but I'm telling you for your own good, it'll be easier once you stop hoping. There's nothing you can do to help her now. And if you keep coming here people will be asking questions about you too – you could lose your job and much more besides. Take my advice, go home, pour yourself a big glass of vodka and go to bed.'

The secret policeman put the parcel down on a bench, looked at it for a moment and left.

A few blocks away, Slovo blew out his candle and curled himself into the usual fetal position he adopted when going to sleep. He had never realised the number of things one had to agree to when falling in love, but Lotya was right; there could be no love until certain matters were taken care of. Of course, he had not taken care of these matters yet, but the point was that he would do so when the time came, of that there could be no doubt. And he would earn Lotya's love while doing so, first on the pitch, and then through leaping on a sleeping body with a cloth, or even by jumping from a cupboard with an axe. He would do both and then live in her love until they grew old. Nothing in his life had ever seemed so straightforward or simple before. It was just a shame that there was this other problem that Kasper had told him about, one that did not just concern him and Lotya, but the whole team. It was difficult to see what the two had to do with each other, but there was no doubt that they might be connected, since if Spartak won a game they had to lose then perhaps neither he nor Lotya would ever see Paris or kill Grotsky. This would make it so much harder to know what to do next, if he chose to explore the problem. Deciding not to, he tucked his head into his chest and fell asleep.

# Chapter Eleven

---

*Friday*

Radek finished reading the letter and stared at it for a moment; it was the fifth of its kind he had written in a week but this one, unlike the others, had been written not in hope but in the confidence that hope was no longer necessary; that what would be would be. This fatalism, given to him in his last dream, was having a strangely liberating effect, and as he read the letter back to himself he realised that, if he was not careful, he could find himself writing a dozen such letters to Katya every week for the rest of his life. He sighed. This would have to be the last. In a few hours' time the rest of the city would be waking up and he would be playing the game of his life. He tried to think of what Katya might be doing at this moment but found that he could not; she was in a different story now, one that he no longer had the power either to imagine or enter. Putting the letter down, he walked confidently across the room and lay down fully clothed on his bed.

He was asleep within a minute, dreaming of scoring goals for the glory of the most beautiful girl in Russia, if not the world.

He woke up to the blare of horns sounding every-where. It was Friday afternoon and Moscow was going crazy. In two hours the city's leading teams were to do battle, and the Muscovites, like anxious parents, were eager to stop lazy players from oversleeping. The banging Radek had thought he had heard in his sleep was in fact coming from his window; a flotilla of snowballs were being hurled at it by what sounded like banshees. He grabbed the window nearest to his bed and flung it open. Above him the sky was coughing up clouds, like clots of blood, and below the crowds were roaring his name, his name and that of his team, and there weren't just a few of them gathered there, *there were thousands*.

'Radek, Radek, Spartak, Spartak.'

Before he had time even to take the scene in he felt a hand on his shoulder; it was Makhno's. 'Come on, Radek, there's a car waiting downstairs. It's time to go.'

Chaos had reigned from the minute Tomsky had arrived at the Spartak building that morning to the moment he realised he would have to leave. All four of the team's buses at the motor pool had been sabotaged, and despite frantic phone calls no one had been able to come up with any replacements. To add to his woes the team had, in the space of a single night, been struck with a personnel crisis, with the second-team defenders Bulgakov and Pasternak being picked up on charges of affray, dating back to the players' party, and Grossman, the Lithuanian centre-half, facing deportation on account of a 'counterfeit' passport.

To compound matters the physio, Timoshenko, had vanished without trace and Koba, having complained of a groin strain, had disappeared with him. Tomsky's task was made no easier by a late phone call from Copic telling him that he would meet the rest of the team at the stadium as his head was in the process of being stitched up. It seemed, if his boss was to be believed, that the hapless Copic had been attacked in his sleep and had been lucky to fight off the assailants without losing his life or, equally plausibly, he had walked into his front door again. This meant that any chance to discuss the game would be, at the very best, confined to a rushed chat on the touchline or a few minutes grabbed in the changing room. Although Copic had seemed keen enough on playing to win after the phone call from Stalin, a lot could have happened in one night, and Tomsky did not like the idea of not having him close at hand.

In every one of their last-minute misfortunes Tomsky could detect the unmistakable hand of the NKVD, and with this understanding came the equally familiar feeling that they, and the world they stood for, could be contained but never beaten. It had been like this for as long as he could remember, but in the past he had been able to console himself with the thought that they would never come for him, because he would never do anything to *make* them come for him. Instead he would leave the heroics to others, keep his head down and, if he was lucky, be forgotten. And yet here he was, not only vying for their attention, but practically demanding it. He smiled; it was amusing to realise what a poor judge he had been of his own nature. Though maybe not just his own but that of the NKVD as well, since he could feel something else too, something new, hopeful and delightfully rare, a sense that the authorities were finally becoming desperate. But this was a feeling that he did not have too much time to appreciate. There was too much to try to get right first.

Beckoning Josip to follow him, he rounded the remaining seven players, who had not already left of their own devices, into a semicircle and pointed at the rusty old vehicle. 'Boys, we have no choice. I've tried everything, and short of commandeering vehicles at gunpoint this old hulk is all I could come up with. We will have to follow the rest of the squad to the stadium in this, or not at all. Are there any questions? No? Good. Sholokhov, are you sure you can drive this? You can? Right, the rest of you pile in.'

Bemused bystanders waved and laughed as Josip bundled the players into the old lorry, unsure whether the confusion unfolding around them was part of an elaborate joke told by the team as a whole, or just some private matter that they, as fans, did not need to concern themselves with.

Slamming the back door shut, Tomsky ran around to the front of the vehicle and climbed into the passenger seat beside Sholokhov, the youth team goalkeeper. 'Will she go, or are we fucked?'

Sholokhov nodded and revved the engine.

'Well, put your foot down, then. We've got just under two hours.'

The old lorry rumbled through the square and on to the long Kalinin expressway leading up to the floodlit Dynamo stadium.

'My God, look at it,' whispered Sholokhov.

The whole length of the expressway was black with people, for once not staring at the frozen river but joining a long procession of torch-bearers and cyclists, their flashlights reflecting off the dark patches of the Volga, whilst high above them the electric grids around the Church of the Ascension flickered like Christmas lights. The unregulated flow of bodies moved with an organising principle of its own, sometimes appearing like a giant chain, and then fragmenting into a thousand individual parts, like a talismanic eagle revelling in its wingspan.

'Put your hand down on the horn and just plough through the middle, or else we'll never get there.'

'Will do.'

'Tomsky,' said Josip, tapping his shoulder.

'What is it?'

'No, nothing else to worry you, I was just wondering about Hubbard. Makhno told me they put him on a plane home and that he'll be shot when he gets back to England.'

'Why bring him up of all people?'

'Well, we both shared the experience of being foreigners in a strange land and that can produce uncommon bonds.' Josip smiled.

'I don't know whether the English will shoot him. Not everyone does things as we do, but I know he's out of the country now, and not likely to come back. Not in this life anyway.'

'It's sad for him. He was obviously mad but he was a character, and on those occasions we spoke he told me he wanted to find out more about life here. Discover the real Russia, he said.'

Tomsky sneered. 'If you really want to find out about this country you'd visit its prison camps, not hang around with its football teams. It took him too long to realise that the name of the game is not cricket out here.'

'I know,' said Josip.

Tomsky looked over his shoulder and tapped the Catalan's arm. 'I know what you're thinking – out of the frying pan and into the fire, or something like that, am I right?'

Josip snorted. 'Would it make any difference if I did? You speak as though I have some kind of choice in this whole affair.'

'Don't you?'

'No. Which is why I feel freer than I ever have before. And besides, when I jump on board a bandwagon I stay on it.'

'Congratulations, Guardiola, you sound like a man who has got the joke in the nick of time!'

Josip laughed and tried to look out of the window; it was no bigger than the portal on the ship that had brought him to Russia. All he could make out was the snake-like procession of bodies, interrupted by the jolting of the lorry's faulty suspension. It was curiously gratifying to know that all these strangers were walking into a giant theatre to watch him, especially as he usually went to such efforts to keep a low profile. It would certainly be something to spend his last hours alive in front of thousands of screaming spectators instead of clinging to driftwood in a burning sea. Josip felt like laughing at his own morbidity. How did he know he was going to die? The fact of the matter was that he didn't and, if he were to be honest with himself, he was actually close to enjoying the occasion, the impending drama appealing to his sense of the ridiculous.

'At least we'll be given a big send-off this way.' He smiled, not sure whether to believe his own pessimism.

'I wouldn't be so sure. They'll probably clear the stadium after our first goal.'

'Just so long as they pronounce my name right this time . . .'

'I hate to disappoint you but I've got a bad feeling you'll make it out of this in one piece, Josip.'

'I know, but it will be so lonely on my own.'

Tomsky laughed nervously. It seemed a fine time to admit to himself that he had no idea what he was doing, no idea whether he or any of the others would live or die, or whether he had chosen to do the right thing. No matter how hard he thought about it, there would only ever be decisions, which, because of their simplicity, rendered the range and detail of his thinking useless. Which was why he had stopped thinking, made his decision and was now worrying.

'Tomsky!'

'What?'

'We're being flagged over. What should I do?'

Tomsky looked out of the window. A large open-top car packed full of decorated commissars was edging the old lorry off the road.

'You know what the trouble with this country is, Sholokhov? Too many chiefs and not enough braves.'

'What's that?'

'Nothing, just an expression I learnt in America. Pull over before they run us off the road.'

Two of the commissars got out of the car; one walked around the old lorry, swinging his baton at it as if to search for some defect, while the other stood shaking his head and reached for some papers in his overcoat.

'What the hell do these two shit-heels want?' muttered Tomsky under his breath. 'How can we be of help, Comrades?' he called from the window.

'Do you have a licence for this vehicle, Comrade?' asked the nearest commissar.

'Not with me. I'm borrowing it off a friend. He has it.'

'No licence, you say. Not good, Comrade, not good at all. You say you're "borrowing" it off a friend. Where can this friend of yours be found?'

'At the Red October Leatherworks, but it's a Spartak

vehicle and, as a member of the union, I'm entitled to drive any union vehicle . . .'

'We can see that from the number plates, Comrade, we're not blind, you know. But that's not the issue here. The problem is you're driving an unlicensed vehicle . . .'

'Without a permit for carrying passengers,' interrupted the second commissar, 'in a vehicle which is, in any case, completely unroadworthy and a danger to public safety. It may have escaped your attention, Comrade, but the streets are full of people. An accident would involve a lot more than just you, your passengers and this clapped-out old hulk. What I'm saying is that an accident could involve the deaths of several innocent civilians. Perhaps you hadn't thought of that, Comrade, in your rush to get to your precious football match?'

'It's old, I'll grant you that, but it was moving along well enough before you stopped us.'

'It was an accident waiting to happen, Comrade. No, no, I'm sorry, but it would be dereliction of our duty to permit you to travel any farther in this vehicle. We have a job to do just as you have.'

The other commissar nodded officiously and pulled a booklet out of his pocket. 'Yes, Comrade, it always starts with small things like this and the next thing you know we're having to deal with the aftermath of a full-blown disaster. Not a pretty thing to clean up, I can assure you.'

Tomsky could feel the time passing like so many birds migrating into the distance. In its place there emerged a grim and agitated panic, telling him that if he didn't act quickly there would be paperwork for him to fill in followed by a trip to the cells.

'You're absolutely right, Comrade Commissioners,' he bellowed from the window. 'I appreciate you stopping me. If you hadn't, and we'd crashed, I could have had the death of seven Spartak players on my conscience.'

The commissars looked startled, as if the fight they had been expecting had turned and vanished at precisely the wrong moment. Moreover a few passing fans had stopped to watch.

'That's Tomsky,' one of them called, 'Tomsky of Spartak. Hey, what are you doing there, Tomsky, we've tickets to see you at the Dynamo in an hour. Our boys are going to kick your hides this time.'

'Only if we get there, lads.'

The first commissar stepped in to try to move the fans along, but more had gathered and the truck was now surrounded by fans of both teams, pushing the commissars to one side and shouting questions at Tomsky, who had climbed down from the truck and was now standing on its roof.

'Listen, boys, the long and short of it is that our truck's broken down and our comrades in the secret police wanted me to ask you if you could give us a lift up to the Dynamo. There's eight of us including me . . .'

'Here, Tomsky,' shouted a snow sweeper, 'you and your boys can ride with us . . .'

Tomsky leapt off the bonnet and landed in a mass of arms and hands. His heart was beating as fast as it had when he had followed Muerta out of the dining hall and kissed her on the steps. He felt in the grip of more than just excitement – something far more like a madness that cared everything for actions and nothing for consequences. Moments earlier he had been afraid of losing Muerta and everything else in his life; now he felt he was moving closer to her by the minute, not just physically but in spirit. His confidence was back; he remembered his conversation with Makhno, the part about how both the choices they faced were bad but one had honour and the other had safety but with strings attached. Was that what they had said? He couldn't remember; he did not care. He looked behind him. Sholokhov and Josip were inches away, pushing through the crowd, and the commissars were nowhere to be seen. Tomsky started to laugh. Things were happening at a speed he wasn't used to.

'Hey, Guardiola.'

'What?'

'Perhaps this is why we Russians get so excited about revolutions!'

'What are you talking about?'

Tomsky didn't answer. Instead he mounted the ledge of the snow sweepers' truck, a converted armoured car, and beckoned to the rest of the team to do the same.

Josip pulled his hat down over his ears; far behind him the Red Star on top of Radio Moscow was glowing like a living torch amidst the dark and falling snow, reminding him of the setting sun that had watched him leave for Barcelona docks, nearly a year ago to the day. He shuddered. He was happy, but it was cold.

Copic cast a nervous eye over the dressing room. Although it was full of bodies, probably only half of them belonged to members of the Spartak first team. His bruised head was throbbing like a radiator and his voice felt stretched and dry. The noise echoing around the room kept burying the game plan he was trying to remember and his good eye kept twitching. In short, he did not consider himself to be the master of the situation.

'At least you got boy wonder Radek here in one piece,' he said to Makhno, 'but where the hell are the others?'

'They'll be here, don't worry. There's still an hour or so to go.'

'Listen, Nestor, I'm not feeling one hundred per cent so I'm going to let you take over here for a while, at least until Tomsky gets here. And you're captain today so . . . so get these shitehawks, and anyone else who isn't involved in the team, out of here while I . . .'

'Igor Ivanovich Copic?'

Copic turned his head with relief; the interruption was a welcome one.

'What is it?' he asked.

The linesman who had poked his head around the door coughed into his hand. 'It's the referee; he would like to see you, outside, if that's possible.'

'Can't it wait?' growled Makhno.

'No, it's all right, I'll see him,' said Copic.

Stepping past the linesman, Copic entered the dimly lit corridor.

'Where is he? I can't see a damn thing.'

'Don't worry, Igor Ivanovich, nor can I,' said Grotsky.

# Chapter Twelve

'Come and walk with me for a while, Copic. We have plenty to talk about.'

'I don't know what gave you that idea, but in case you've missed the fact, I've a team I need to prepare for a match of no small consequence . . .'

'And so have I, Copic, so have I . . . but I'm sure our two teams will be able to cope in our absence . . . it's about time they did, don't you think?'

'I don't know how you run yours, Grotsky, but I like to have a hands-on relationship with mine. It's why we win things, you see – I have no conflict of interest, I just run a football team and that's it. You . . . well, you have other things to do.'

'This is exactly what I mean! Look at us, standing here asking each other all these questions. We interest each other, admit it!'

'I admit that I have no idea why you'd want to talk to me now, rather than at the post-match drink that you've never once bothered coming to.'

'Then give me this chance to put it right! Here, follow me.'

Grotsky walked to the end of the corridor and pushed open a part of the wall, which he stepped through. Copic followed him into what appeared to be either a very small changing room or a holding cell. The cramped space was lit by a single phosphorescent lamp, nailed to the wall next to a small photograph of a young woman.

Grotsky sat down on the tiny wooden bench and took off his cap.

'Welcome to my meditative space,' he said, waving his arm over his head with a half-hearted flourish.

Copic stared at him with a mixture of distaste and curiosity. It was hard to think of the last occasion on which they had actually seen each other, let alone talked to one another. Normally Copic would stand at one end of the dugout and Grotsky at the other, perhaps exchanging the odd glance as they rose from the bench, but nothing more. The physical similarities between the two men had often been commented on, but what Copic felt as he glared at Grotsky went beyond mere recognition of oneself in another. Copic was reminded of an incident by the Black Sea where, as a child, he had seen a boy he had mistaken for himself. Copic had watched with intense interest, sure that if he looked hard enough he would find some difference, as indeed he did, but not before a whole hour had passed and the boy had come out of the water to ask Copic what he was looking at. It was then that Copic realised he was a full foot taller than the boy and that, when he spoke, the boy's words came out of the side of his mouth, whereas Copic's flew out of the front of his. It was this same inner resemblance Copic could see in Grotsky, though, as he looked more carefully, this identification was mitigated by a number of crucial differences. For one thing, even though Grotsky was in better shape than Copic, he still looked the sicker of the two men, his eyes covered in a pallid layer of sleep residue. The rest of his face was pasty and tinged with grey, as if it had been constructed from glue and old newspaper. There was also a forced quality to every movement which suggested that anything natural, be it the lifting of a hand or the pleasure taken in hearing a morning chorus, was anathema to Grotsky. His limbs seemed like a great weight dropped on him, and his voice an inadequate tool with which to deal with this curse. Copic smiled; it looked as if Grotsky was not enjoying his life.

'So what do you want to talk about, Klimt?'

'Us, Copic, I want to talk about us. You used to like talking, don't you remember? You were even quite articulate if I remember rightly, always piling in on those silly debates we used to hold after our evening classes. You remember those? Always trying out the new expressions and words you'd learnt the hour before . . .'

'I'll be relieved if a talk's all you're after, but somehow I don't think it is.'

'And maybe ask you a few questions as well.'

'Ever the secret policeman.'

Grotsky chuckled quietly and cleared his throat. 'Do you know what a tragicomedy is, Igor Ivanovich?'

'A comedy that no one finds funny?'

'No. A drama where the gay and the sad are blended. You and I, we form something of a tragicomedy, don't you think? All of us old ones do, I with blood on my hands, Gorky with blood in his ink, and you with blood on your laces. And every one of us enjoying enough lives to keep a cat happy.'

'What are you building up to?'

'That we all, at some point or another, have compromised our consciences for the benefit of a greater good. And that this is what holds Russians of our generation, great Russians of our generation, together.'

'I must say that I'm surprised to hear you talk about conscience . . .'

'Why?'

'Because the last time I mentioned the subject you didn't seem to have much time for it. No time for it at all, in fact. The trial of Rebrov, the Marathon swimmer? You don't remember? The petition you wanted me to sign condemning him to death? You were pretty keen on the subject, if I remember rightly, on how there are no consciences any more; only class instincts. "We live entirely on the outside, we have abolished the inside." Doesn't that ring any bells?'

Grotsky snorted. 'You should have been a politician, Copic. You missed your true calling when you became a footballer. I'll be straight with you – you're like the bear that pisses in the mountain stream, stirs it up, and then expects all the other animals to drink from it. But we others, we *have* to drink from it. But whatever *you* don't like the taste of, you close your eyes to, and yet you still want to help yourself to seconds when it suits you. Haven't you ever considered your selective vision to be nothing if not hypocritical? Or don't you full-time football managers use long words like that?'

'No, you're right, Grotsky. Perhaps I like not seeing things as they really are. To perceive life as it actually is in this place is to go mad, but to believe that it was true, that this reality we've constructed is anything more than a gross circus act, that would be even madder still. And yet to deny it is to risk death and still not be able to do anything about it. Which is why I prefer games. Anything over debasing myself in front of the cult of power like the rest of you badge-wearers.'

'Catch my lice, Copic! That's humanist piss if ever I've heard it.'

'Better piss than your Party and all its twisted jargon. It's gone so far into your system that you forget that some of us would rather do without it.'

'Damn you, don't you confuse me with some hack. You'll never hear us old ones talk in the official "jargon", as you call it. That's a young man's game. The minute they're on duty, which is just about every minute of their precious lives, you'll hear them speak it; it's the only language they know. Why, they probably even think that their pricks belong to the state,' snapped Grotsky, frustrated at having been led off the point.

'And whose fault is that?'

'What do you expect me to do about it – scream your humanist mantra under the Kremlin walls so Stalin changes his mind about historical necessity just so he can catch a good night's sleep? You just haven't learnt it yet, have you? *Nothing does any good any more*. Sure, things would have been better if we were other than what we are, and what we are is a lot worse than what we were, but I leave that kind of thought to the rebels, clowns and loners slopping out on the archipelago.'

'It's strange, Klimt. Listening to you doesn't make me think that I'm listening to the self-proclaimed King of Moscow . . .'

'You idiot! That's just my point. It's not about individuals and free will any more, it's about the masses and history and none of us, not even the Boss, can do anything about it now. I have power, sure, but not in the way a deluded fool like you imagines it. The Tsar was shot years ago. Men don't make history by themselves through some effort of the will in this day and age. And you're a stubborn bastard for believing they still do.'

'Why? Because I'm not caught by my balls like you . . .'

'No. Because you think there's something noble about resisting the course of history and acting like you have a will of your own. Don't you remember? We were all brought up to believe in destiny. That each of us had a path preordained for us, one that we had no control over? So what's so different about what I'm saying to you now?'

'You're right, I do have a destiny, but you're wrong to believe that it's the same one as yours, or anyone else's for that matter,' said Copic, rising to the occasion.

'It's a destiny which recognises my freedom to choose my own destiny . . .'

'Don't try this sophistry out on me, Copic. I thought you'd given it up, and besides, it doesn't suit you and I don't have the time or taste for it now. You know, you may hate me but at least I know your world, even though I reject it. The ones that follow me will know nothing at all. But I digress; I'm here to make you a proposition, one that you'd be wise to listen to so long as your pride doesn't get in the way . . .'

'Is this a business proposition or a sporting one?'

'It's me trying to help you. That's why I asked to see you like this, why I thought it would be better for us to meet alone, to save embarrassing you in front of your team, but also because I want this to be a truly sporting occasion – at least for the first half. But in the second half, I tell you, you'll play to lose. Failure to do so will not just be an insult to me, which is what you mistakenly seem to think this is all about, but an insult to the Soviet state and to anything we still hold in common and have ever aligned ourselves with.'

'As I have no idea what that might be, you may as well speak plainly and get to the point,' said Copic, sounding as though he were almost enjoying himself. 'You want us to throw the game, that's it, isn't it? All the rest of this rhetoric's just gloss . . .'

'Don't adopt that tone with me, Copic,' shouted Grotsky. 'I could have you and that wretched team of yours machine-gunned in the foot baths if I so chose.'

'If nothing's stopping you then why the hell don't you do it?'

Grotsky glared at Copic and bit the end of his thumb, angry that he was allowing himself to be led off the subject again. 'I live in a house built on dog shit and tiled in worry. Your death isn't even worth the paperwork.'

'That's what you'd have me believe, isn't it? Maybe you're right, Klimt, maybe it's really true and you aren't as powerful as you think and all this talk is just a nice wordy justification of that simple fact. My death isn't even worth the paperwork to you, eh? Is that what you think, or is that what your hero in the Kremlin left in your in-tray today? Listening to you wouldn't be half as bad as it is if I actually thought you strayed into your own opinions now and then. But you don't, not even by mistake. It's the same with all of you secret policemen – the minute Stalin shits you gentlemen offer your handkerchiefs . . .'

'Shut your fucking mouth! Do you really think I like that pockmarked bastard any more than you do? Do you think he really won't be coming for my head one day once he's finished with the others? He'll kill any and he'll kill all who can remember who he was before he became our great leader. Everyone from his former life is a threat to be done away with, anyone who's actually seen him in the flesh and knows how little he is, and how small he was before he awarded himself all those titles . . .'

'Is that a fact . . .'

'Of course it isn't. It's an opinion. Even you should have grasped that minds are not made up of facts but of beliefs, and each belief is just an opinion. Facts are for scientists or Christians, and the camps are full of both.' Grotsky wiped the sweat off his head and looked at his watch. 'Choose life over death, Copic. Bring them in at half-time and tell them to throw the game. They love you and will do as you say. You don't even need to explain anything to them.'

'I won't.'

'What?'

'I said no.'

'Are you mad? Are you really so mad as to not have understood anything I've told you? I'm giving you a chance, which is more than anyone else would give you. If you don't do as I ask you will die. Surely that must mean something, even to a dumb shit-loving pig like yourself.'

'There's no love lost between us, is there, Klimt?'

'Mother of Kazan, Copic, I'm serious. Don't try and call my bluff. If you think that by somehow sacrificing yourself you'll be able to take me down with you, then I assure you that you've never been more wrong. Since our people took over time has stopped and you . . . well, you'll become one more statistic just like the rest of the camp dust. You'll end up toe to toe with your sons, Copic, dead and forgotten. There'll be no coming back to name us, your executioners, just the long night to be slept through for ever. Mark these words, Igor Ivanovich, and mark them well.' Grotsky got up off the bench and wiped his damp hands along the seams of his trousers. 'So what do you say? Do you accept my offer?'

Copic sighed and shook his head, his gait not dissimilar to that of a peasant dithering over the sale of a horse. 'As you say, Klimt, this is Russia, and any road I choose is certain to bring disaster. You were right to point out that, whereas you've learnt the important lessons, I've just let them pass me by . . .'

'Don't play the coy village idiot with me . . .'

'Not least that anything is possible, if it's possible by trickery. But the trouble is, once the shouting is over, I'm an honest man.'

'It's simple, Copic, you just have to say yes or no. And let there be no more confusion. If you say no I'll make you and your team suffer for it. I still have the power to.'

'Hasn't it occurred to you, Klimt, that we might be two people who'll never have a moment as good as this again?'

Grotsky looked at Copic as a veterinary surgeon would a rabid dog before a lethal injection. 'I don't understand. What are you talking about?'

'I'm tired, Grotsky, I don't want to make my team act like a branch of state policy, or as you would make the whole country behave . . .'

'Which is how?'

'To put more real and genuine impulses to dishonest uses.'

'I thought I'd made you understand . . .'

'No, it's you who don't understand. You don't understand that when my players go out they're not just playing for themselves, their club, for me or even for each other. When they play they see what I do, the faces of dead sons and loved ones, burnt wheat fields and dry rivers, man-made famines and much more besides. And one poor bastard even plays for a woman who doesn't love him any more. So you see, it's you who don't understand when you ask me to do this thing for you. This is heart and honour, Klimt, our way of holding on until there's nothing left to hold on to, always with the lasting satisfaction that we were the ones who never let go. As you've said before, it's us old ones who survived the Civil War who understand this impulse best, that life is never so valuable or rich as it is when we realise it won't last.'

'Life is not a value, Igor Ivanovich – it is a delayed reaction to the inevitable. You choose death; so be it. I was a fool ever to believe in your intelligence. Now get out of my way.'

Copic stepped out of Grotsky's path and let the secret policeman brush past him. To his surprise he did not close and lock the door behind him but, after waiting in the shadows for a second, cursed and disappeared into the corridor.

Copic left the room in a better mood than when he had walked into it. His head felt clearer and his hands had stopped shaking; his back felt as if a lance had been pulled out of it. Treading lightly for once, he floated down the corridor like a cloud disappearing before rain. The strong smell of chlorine and floor polish, which usually evoked unpleasant memories of his wife's death in hospital, now reminded him of the fun they had together, as he taught her to hold and pass the ball all those years ago outside the little flat they all shared in Leningrad. His whole body felt very much at the mercy of an organ it often had difficulty in locating; his heart.

He could hear a great deal of good-natured yelling coming from behind the closed door of the Spartak dressing room. Careful not to disturb the yeller's rhythm, he prised open the door and took in the spectacle. In his absence, Makhno had very much taken control, and was approaching the closing stages of a team talk that had, in all likelihood, not dwelt much on the technical aspects of the game.

'The very hard core of the games-playing elite is who we are; you ask me what does that mean? Well, I'll tell you, boys, the hard core is not being scared of the consequences of the truth, and the truth is that, out of Spartak and Dynamo, we're the hard core and they're a shower of shit, so let's make them run, boys, because we're faster than they are and that's the truth. So let's get behind the boss and act as one mind.'

Copic nodded approvingly; it had not happened overnight but they were learning at last. Quickly he ran his eyes over those faces closest to the door: Uritsky the sweeper, Sverdlov the winger, Rykov the centre-half and Serge the right back. Makhno was right, they really did all appear to be of one mind. Only Slovo seemed a little out of joint, but then, Copic mused, he always did. Not wishing to interrupt Makhno's climax, if indeed he had climaxed, Copic gently closed the door, the very picture of a benevolent Santa Claus. It had taken a long time for his team to operate without him, and if that meant they no longer needed him then it was all to the good. An ego did not befit a man old enough to have fathered their girlfriends, and who had trouble getting out of his trousers at night.

Having climbed to the top of the stairs, to the point where they led on to the players' tunnel, Copic began to come down to earth again, but not so much as to be intimidated by the huge roar he could now hear. The noise coming from the stadium, and travelling through the tunnel, was awesome, like the thunderous volley of the artillery battery he had commanded during the Civil War. Not waiting for the team to join him, Copic walked through alone, his mind the property of pure bewilderment.

Nothing from his playing days could prepare him for what he saw next. It was as if God had created a world small enough to fit into a football stadium. The light outside was blinding, and for a minute all Copic could see were giant lake-size spots, smothering his vision like an eclipse. Rows of anti-aircraft searchlights lit up the pitch, which looked large enough for at least four teams. Behind them watchtowers loomed like ogres angry at having been woken up; it was funny that Copic had never noticed these before, though whether they had always been there, or had just been put up, he did not know. To his right, immediately above the Dynamo dugout, sat a row of pistol-carrying NKVD men, synchronised like the arm of a long leather jacket, their expressions strangely relaxed despite their intermittent sneering. In the middle of them, perched like a valuable mascot, was Grotsky's Lotya, her face looking oddly seasick.

The first twenty rows nearest the Spartak dugout were full of Civil War orphans, the proud winners of a state-sponsored collective lottery, their discordant howls echoing down the corridor like a flock of low-flying owls. Between them and the main stand, reserved for the Party leadership, sat Zayets and Rykhly, their faces passive and unreadable. Copic decided that it would be better not to wave, and turned round to face friendlier sights.

Over on the far side of the stadium, reaching right up to the gods and making the most of the noise, were the Spartak faithful – the factory workers, the embittered intelligentsia and the scum of the Vendee; those happy few who would sooner hold in a piss for ninety minutes than miss a second of the game. And far behind them stood patches of green and brown, the starving peasants who had just arrived in the city and who had chosen the spectacle over the search for food, work or lodgings.

It all looked like a painting Josip had shown him from a Spanish book on art, in which all the models had been ordinary people who, knowing that they would return to their own lives the following day, were determined to make full use of their borrowed ones while they still could. It was at once both an affirmation and an exaggeration of life, unreal and yet impossible to wake up from, like a shared dream that all the spectators had to take part in, in order to discover the truth of.

'Hey, boss, apologies for our lateness, but if you'd been through what we have, you'd give us points for getting here at all.'

It was Tomsky, laughing like a schoolboy, as he barged through the crowd and leapt over the barriers like a hurdler. With him were Josip and some of the reserve players, who threw themselves on their backs and changed frantically out of their tracksuits on the touchline.

'Been through what you have? You schnapps-loving milksops! More like been through what I have!' said Copic, tapping his bandaged head. 'Get your arses over here, and get them into gear sharpish. The rest of the lads will be out in a minute. I don't know who they were planning to put in for Josip and Martov in midfield, but they'll see we've returned to Plan A once they've clocked that you clowns have shown at last.'

'You'll have to speak up, boss, I can hardly hear a word you're saying over the noise.'

Copic repeated himself, this time shouting out every word at the top of his voice, but it was no good, nothing could be heard over the rising din. Both teams were coming on to the pitch and a figure that Copic took to be Stalin had stood up in the middle tier and was saluting the players. Out of the corner of his eye Copic spotted the chesty figure of Radek's Katya standing among the orphans; she was singing, singing with forty thousand others who, like her, were waving clumps of red-and-white cloth in time to 'The Internationale'. He held his hand to his face.

It would not be long now before he would know whether it had all been worth it.

Waving at the screaming children, Copic walked over to the Dynamo dugout and offered his hand to Grotsky, who refused it with a scowl.

The referee blew his whistle, Radek kicked the ball back to Makhno, and the game began.

\*      \*      \*      \*      \*      \*      \*

# Acknowledgements

For the true, and more incredible, story of Spartak and Dynamo (one that does not take the considerable historical, geographical and linguistical liberties that I have) I recommend my old tutor Jim Riordan's article 'The Strange Story of Nikolai Starostin, Football and Lavrenti Beria' in *Europe-Asia Studies*, vol. 46, no. 4, 1994. Unlike many stories of the period, this one has a happy ending.

The poet who appears in the Spartak party scene misquotes from Osip Mandelstam's 'We are alive but no longer feel', *The Moscow Notebooks*, Bloodaxe Books, 1991.

Thank you, Helen Garnons-Williams and Jocasta Brownlee at Sceptre, Eugenie Furniss and Lucinda Prain at William Morris, and all those friends who read *Homage* and encouraged me during the writing of this.